Into the
Abyss

Elizabeth Chappelle

Hummingbird Publishing Ltd

Contents

Chapter 1

Dr. Evelyn Hartley stood on the deck of the research vessel Nautilus; her eyes locked on the endless expanse of the Atlantic Ocean. The sea was deceptively calm, a vast, glittering blue that stretched out in every direction, merging seamlessly with the sky at the horizon. But Evelyn wasn't fooled by its serene appearance. She knew that beneath the surface lay a world of darkness and danger, a place where the rules of nature were twisted and strange.

The wind whipped through her hair, which she had tied back in a loose ponytail that now fluttered against her back like a banner. She closed her eyes for a moment, letting the salty breeze wash over her, the familiar scent of the sea bringing a brief sense of comfort and romantic, foreboding. The ocean had always been her sanctuary, a place where she felt at home. But today, that feeling was overshadowed by a gnawing sense of unease that she couldn't shake.

As she opened her eyes, she caught her reflection in the

glass of the ship's cabin window. Her face was stern, with high cheekbones and a strong jawline that spoke of her determination. Her skin, naturally fair, had taken on a slight tan from years of exposure to the elements. But it was her eyes deep green and sharp as a hawk's that held the most intensity. They were the eyes of a woman who had spent her life searching for answers, often in places where few dared to look.

Her colleagues often said that she was driven, almost to a fault. It wasn't far from the truth. Evelyn had spent her entire career pushing the boundaries of what was known, venturing into the deepest parts of the ocean to uncover its secrets. The mysteries of the sea fascinated her, but this time, her mission was different. It wasn't just about curiosity or discovery. It was about finding out what had happened to Flight 753.

The plane had vanished without a trace three weeks ago, and despite the most extensive search and rescue operation in recent history, no one had been able to find it. The incident had captured the world's attention, reigniting old fears about the Bermuda Triangle a place where, according to legend, ships and planes disappeared under mysterious circumstances.

Evelyn had never been one to indulge in superstition. As a scientist, she believed in facts, in data that could be analysed and evaluate Yet, as she stood on the deck of the Nautilus, she couldn't ignore the small, insistent voice at the back of her mind that whispered of danger. The Bermuda Triangle had always been a source of fascination for her, but now, it felt like something more like a challenge, a puzzle that needed to be solved.

She turned to look at the crew working around her, their movements brisk and efficient as they prepared for the mission ahead. The Nautilus was an ultramodern research vessel, equipped with the latest technology for oceanographic exploration. Its crew was composed of seasoned sailors and top scientists, all of whom had been handpicked for this expedition. They were professionals, used to the dangers of the sea, but even they seemed to be on edge.

Evelyn had noticed the tension among the crew from the moment they had set sail from Miami. It was in the way they moved, in the hushed conversations she overheard in the mess hall, where the usual camaraderie had been replaced by a sombre silence. She had caught snippets of their discussions about the Bermuda Triangle, about the ships and planes that had disappeared there over the years, and about the fear that they were venturing into a place where the natural laws didn't apply.

She had tried to reassure them, reminding them that they were here to conduct a scientific investigation, that there was no such thing as a cursed stretch of ocean. But deep down, she knew that her words had done little to dispel their fears. And perhaps, if she were honest with herself, she wasn't entirely convinced either.

The sun was beginning to set, casting long shadows across the deck. The sky was a brilliant canvas of oranges and pinks, the kind of sunset that would have taken Evelyn's breath away on any other day. But now, it only served to deepen her sense of foreboding. The beauty of the scene felt like a cruel joke, a fleeting moment of calm before the storm.

She looked out at the horizon, where the deep blue of the ocean met the sky in a sharp line. Somewhere out there, Flight 753 had disappeared. It was hard to believe that something so large, so solid, could simply vanish without a trace. The ocean was vast, yes, but it wasn't infinite. There had to be an explanation, a logical, scientific reason for what had happened.

Evelyn turned her back on the sunset and walked toward the bridge, where Captain James Harris stood at the helm. Captain Harris was a tall man in his late fifties, with a weathered face that bore the marks of a life spent at sea. His hair, once dark, was now streaked with grey, and his blue eyes held the quiet confidence of a man who had seen it all. Evelyn had worked with Harris on several expeditions before, and she trusted him implicitly.

"Captain," she greeted him, stepping into the bridge.

"Dr. Hartley," Harris replied with a nod, his eyes never leaving the horizon. "We're nearing the coordinates you provided. I thought you'd want to be ready."

"Thank you, Captain," Evelyn said, her voice steady despite the tension that coiled in her stomach.

Harris turned to look at her, his expression unreadable. "Are you sure about this, Dr. Hartley? The weather reports aren't looking good. We might be sailing into something we're not prepared for."

Evelyn met his gaze, her green eyes unwavering. "We must find out what happened to that plane, Captain. If there's a chance that we can bring some answers to the families of those who were lost, we owe it to them to try."

Captain Harris nodded slowly, but Evelyn could see the doubt in his eyes. "I've been sailing these waters for over thirty years, Doctor. I've seen things out here that would make a man question his sanity. I'm not a superstitious man, but the Bermuda Triangle… there's something about this place that's different."

Evelyn had heard similar sentiments from others who had sailed through these waters. They spoke of strange lights in the sky, of compasses that spun wildly, and of ships that sailed into the mist and were never seen again. But she had always dismissed these stories as the product of overactive imaginations, fuelled by the fear of the unknown.

But now, standing here on the deck of the Nautilus, with the sun dipping below the horizon and the darkness closing in, she wasn't so sure.

"I understand your concerns, Captain," she said finally, "but we're here to find the truth. Whatever that may be."

Harris sighed, rubbing a hand across his stubbled chin. "Aye, Doctor. But sometimes, the truth isn't what we want it to be."

As they approached the coordinates where the last known signal from Flight 753 had been recorded, the air grew thick with tension. The sky, once painted in vivid hues, had turned a deep, inky black, and the first stars had begun to appear. The ship's powerful floodlights cut through the darkness, illuminating the churning waters below. But even with the lights, the ocean seemed to stretch on endlessly, an abyss that threatened to swallow them whole.

"Prepare to deploy the ROV," Evelyn ordered, her voice cutting through the quiet murmur of the crew.

The remotely operated vehicle was a marvel of modern engineering, equipped with high-definition cameras, advanced sonar, and a suite of sensors designed to detect even the slightest changes in the environment. It was their best chance of finding any trace of the missing plane, or at least, of understanding what had happened to it.

The crew moved quickly, their hands steady despite the tension in the air. Evelyn watched as the ROV was lowered into the water, its cameras coming to life as it descended into the depths. The images began to stream onto the monitor in front of her grainy at first, then sharpening into clear, crisp footage of the ocean floor.

As the ROV descended, Evelyn's breath caught in her throat. The seabed was over 5,000 meters below the surface, a place of eternal darkness where few had ventured. The lights on the ROV revealed a landscape that was both beautiful and alien, with jagged rocks and strange formations that looked like they had been sculpted by a hand far more ancient than any human civilization.

For a moment, Evelyn forgot her fear, her eyes glued to the screen. This was what she lived for the thrill of discovery, the chance to see something that no one else had seen before. But her excitement was tempered by the knowledge of what they were searching for. Somewhere in these depths, she hoped to find the wreckage of Flight 753. But what if she found something else? Something that defied explanation?

As the ROV continued its descent, the tension on the deck grew palpable. The crew watched the monitors with bated breath, their faces illuminated by the eerie glow of the screens. The only sound was the hum of the ship's engines and the occasional crackle of static over the radio.

"Captain, are you seeing this?" Evelyn asked, her voice tight with a mixture of excitement and dread.

"Aye," Harris replied, his eyes narrowing as he studied the readings on his own monitor. "We're picking up an unusual magnetic anomaly, right where the plane went down."

Evelyn frowned, her mind racing. Magnetic anomalies were not uncommon in the deep ocean, where the Earth's magnetic field could be distorted by various factors. But this one was different stronger, more erratic. It was as if the anomaly was alive, shifting and pulsing with a strange energy.

"Could it be a natural phenomenon?" she asked, more to herself than to the captain. "Or something else?"

Harris didn't answer, and Evelyn could tell that he was just as baffled as she was. The readings on the monitor continued to fluctuate, the numbers jumping wildly as the ROV moved closer to the source of the anomaly.

Then, just as suddenly as it had started, the interference stopped.

The feed stabilized, and the image on the monitor cleared.

"What the hell…?" one of the crew members muttered, leaning in closer to the screen.

Evelyn's heart skipped a beat as she saw what the cameras had picked up. The ROV's lights had revealed something large and metallic, half-buried in the silt on the ocean floor. It was twisted and broken, but there was no mistaking what it was the wreckage of an airplane.

"Bring it in closer," Evelyn ordered, her voice barely above a whisper.

The ROV moved forward, its cameras zooming in on the twisted metal. As the lights swept over the wreckage, Evelyn felt a chill run down her spine. The plane's fuselage was crumpled and torn, as if it had been crushed by some immense force. The windows were shattered, and the wings were nowhere to be seen, likely ripped off by the impact.

But what struck Evelyn the most was the eerie stillness of the scene. There were no signs of life, no bodies, no luggage, nothing to suggest that this had once been a plane full of passengers. It was as if the ocean had swallowed them whole, leaving only the shattered remains of the aircraft behind.

"This can't be right," she murmured, more to herself than to anyone else. "There should be something, anything left behind."

"Maybe the current carried it away," Harris suggested, though his voice lacked conviction. "Or maybe… there was nothing left to find."

Evelyn shook her head, her mind racing. The wreckage should have told a story of the plane's ultimate moments, of the passengers who had been on board. But instead, it was like a ghost, a shadow of what it once was.

And then, as she stared at the monitor, something else caught her eye. A dark shape, barely visible on the edge of the camera's range, moving through the water. It was too large to be a fish, and it moved too deliberately to be a piece of debris.

"Did you see that?" she asked, her voice rising with alarm.

The crew exchanged uneasy glances, their eyes darting to the monitor. But the shape was gone, lost in the darkness of the deep.

"What was it?" Harris asked, his voice tense.

"I don't know," Evelyn replied, her heart pounding in her chest. "But whatever it was, it wasn't supposed to be here."

She leaned closer to the monitor, her eyes scanning the screen for any sign of movement. But the ROV's cameras showed only the wreckage of the plane and the dark, empty ocean around it.

"Bring the ROV back up," she ordered, her voice trembling slightly. "We've seen enough for now."

The crew moved quickly, retracting the ROV's cables and bringing it back to the surface. Evelyn watched as the vehicle emerged from the water, its cameras still rolling, but there was nothing more to see. The deep, dark ocean had once again hidden its secrets and decide to send it back down once they have downloaded the data.

As the ROV was secured on deck, Evelyn took a deep breath, trying to steady her nerves. She had seen many strange things in her career, but this was different. There was something about this place, something that defied explanation. The Bermuda Triangle had always been a place of mystery, but now, standing here on the deck of the Nautilus, Evelyn couldn't shake the feeling that she was in over her head.

She turned to Captain Harris, who was watching her with a concerned expression. "What do you think, Doctor?" he asked quietly.

"I don't know," Evelyn admitted, her voice barely above a whisper. "But whatever is happening here, it's not natural."

Harris nodded slowly, his eyes scanning the horizon. "Do you think we should continue?"

Evelyn hesitated, her mind racing. Every instinct she had was telling her to turn back, to leave this place and never return. But she knew that she couldn't she had to find out what had happened to Flight 753, no matter the cost.

"Yes," she said finally, her voice firm. "We continue. We must know the truth and send the ROV back down."

Harris gave her a long, measured look, then nodded. "Aye, Doctor. We'll continue. But I hope you're ready for what we might find."

Evelyn wasn't sure if she was ready. But she knew that she had no choice.

As the Nautilus stayed anchored in the Bermuda Triangle, the ocean around them seemed to change as they lower the ROV into the dark waters which was almost black, the air took on a strange, electric quality that made the hair on the back of Evelyn's neck stand up. The crew grew quieter, their faces tense as they went about their duties. Even the ship's instruments seemed to be affected, with the compass spinning erratically and the radios cutting in and out.

Evelyn stood at the bow of the ship, staring out into the darkness. She couldn't shake the feeling that they were being watched that something was lurking just beneath the surface, waiting for the right moment to strike.

"Dr. Hartley?" a voice called out, breaking her from her thoughts.

She turned to see one of the crew members, a young man named Tommy, approaching her. He was one of the junior scientists on the expedition, fresh out of university and eager to prove himself. But now, he looked pale and nervous, his eyes wide with fear.

"Yes, Tommy?" Evelyn asked, trying to keep her voice calm.

"I… I just wanted to say that I'm with you, Doctor," he stammered, his voice shaking. "I know this is dangerous, but I believe in what we're doing. We must find out what happened."

Evelyn smiled, touched by his sincerity. "Thank you, Tommy. That means a lot."

He nodded, his expression softening slightly. "I just hope… I just hope we find some answers."

"So do I, Tommy," Evelyn replied, her gaze drifting back to the dark water below. "So do I."

As the night wore on, the storm that had been predicted finally arrived. The wind picked up, howling through the rigging and sending waves crashing against the hull of the ship. The sky was lit up by flashes of lightning, illuminating the dark clouds that loomed overhead. The Nautilus was tossed about like a toy, its crew struggling to keep the ship on course.

Evelyn gripped the railing, her knuckles white as she braced herself against the wind. The storm was fierce, but she had weathered worse in her career. What worried her more was the strange behaviour of the ship's instruments. The compass continued to spin wildly, and the radar was picking up strange signals that didn't match any known patterns.

"Captain, what's happening?" she shouted over the roar of the wind, making her way to the bridge.

Harris was at the helm, his face grim as he fought to keep the ship steady. "I don't know, Doctor. The instruments are going haywire. It's like the whole area is saturated with electromagnetic interference."

Evelyn's heart raced as she looked at the screens. The radar was showing blips that appeared and disappeared at random, and the ship's navigation system was struggling to maintain a stable course. It was as if they were sailing through a field of magnetic mines, each one throwing off their readings.

"We need to get out of here," Harris said, his voice strained. "This storm is bad enough without the instruments going crazy."

"No!" Evelyn shouted; her voice filled with a sudden desperation. "We can't leave yet. We're close to something, I can feel it."

Harris shot her a disbelieving look, but Evelyn held her ground. "Captain, please. Just give me a little more time."

Harris hesitated; his eyes locked on hers. Then, with a resigned sigh, he nodded. "Alright, Doctor. But we need to move fast."

Evelyn nodded, her heart pounding as she turned back to the screens. She knew that she was taking a huge risk, but she couldn't leave without knowing what was out there. The wreckage of Flight 753 had been just the beginning there was something else, something that had drawn them here.

As the storm raged on, the Nautilus pressed forward, cutting through the churning waves. The crew worked tirelessly; their fear forgotten as they focused on their tasks. But despite their efforts, the ship continued to struggle against the unseen forces that seemed to be pulling them deeper into the Triangle.

And then, just as suddenly as it had started, the storm began to subside. The wind died down, the waves calmed, and the sky began to clear. But the sense of unease that had settled over the ship remained, as if the storm had been only a prelude to something far more terrifying.

"Dr. Hartley, you need to see this," one of the crew members called out, his voice filled with awe.

Evelyn hurried over to the monitor, her breath catching in her throat as she saw what the cameras had picked up. The ROV had found something a massive structure, half-buried in the silt on the ocean floor.

It was unlike anything she had ever seen before. The structure was ancient, covered in strange markings and overgrown with coral and seaweed. It looked like a temple, or perhaps a tomb, and it radiated an aura of power that made the hair on the back of her neck stand on end.

"What... what is it?" Tommy asked, his voice trembling with fear.

Evelyn shook her head, unable to tear her eyes away from the screen. "I don't know. But whatever it is, it's not natural."

The ROV moved closer, its lights revealing more details of the structure. The markings on the walls were intricate, almost hypnotic, and they seemed to pulse with a faint, eerie glow. There were symbols that Evelyn didn't recognize, but they felt strangely familiar, as if she had seen them somewhere before.

And then, as the ROV reached the entrance of the structure, the feed suddenly cut out. The screen went black, and the ship was plunged into silence.

"What happened?" Harris demanded; his voice filled with urgency.

"I don't know," one of the technicians replied, frantically trying to restore the feed. "We've lost contact with the ROV."

Evelyn's heart raced as she stared at the blank screen. The ROV was their only link to the depths below, and without it, they were blind. She had a sinking feeling that whatever they had found down there, it didn't want to be disturbed.

"We need to bring the ROV back up," Harris said, his voice tense. "We can't afford to lose it."

Evelyn nodded, her mind racing. They had come so far, and now, just as they were on the verge of a breakthrough, it felt like everything was slipping away.

"Do it," she said finally, her voice heavy with resignation.

The crew worked quickly, but as they tried to retract the ROV's cables, they found that something was wrong. The cables were stuck, as if they were caught on something deep below the surface.

"It's not budging," one of the crew members said, his voice strained. "It's like something's holding it down."

Evelyn felt a chill run down her spine. "What do you mean?"

"I don't know, Doctor. But whatever it is, it's not letting go."

The crew continued to struggle with the cables, but no matter what they did, the ROV remained stuck. It was as if the structure below was holding it captive, refusing to let it go.

"We're going to lose it," Harris said, his voice filled with frustration.

"No," Evelyn whispered, her eyes locked on the black screen. "We can't."

But despite their efforts, the cables began to fray, and with a final, agonizing snap, they broke free. The ROV was gone, lost to the depths below.

Evelyn stood there in stunned silence, her heart heavy with defeat. They had come so close, only to lose everything in the end. The mystery of the Bermuda Triangle had claimed yet another victim, and this time, it was them.

As the ship turned back toward the open ocean, leaving the Triangle behind, Evelyn couldn't shake the feeling that they had only just scratched the surface of something far greater and far more dangerous than they had ever imagined.

And as they sailed away, the strange, ancient structure lay buried in the darkness, its secrets hidden once again.

For now.

Chapter 2

The morning sun struggled to pierce through the thick veil of mist that clung stubbornly to the surface of the ocean. The Nautilus rocked gently on the calm waters, its once-pristine white hull now bearing the scars of the previous night's tempest. The air was heavy with a damp chill, and a palpable sense of unease hung over the vessel like an unwelcome spectre.

Dr. Evelyn Hartley stood alone on the aft deck; her hands wrapped tightly around a steaming mug of black coffee. Dark circles underscored her weary green eyes, evidence of a sleepless night haunted by questions and doubts. She gazed out at the endless expanse of grey, her mind replaying the events of the previous day in an incessant loop.

The loss of the ROV weighed heavily on her conscience. It wasn't just a piece of equipment; it was their lifeline to the mysteries concealed beneath the ocean's surface. Losing it felt like a personal failure, a door to the unknown slammed shut before she could fully glimpse what lay beyond.

She took a tentative sip from her mug, the bitter liquid doing little to chase away the lingering fatigue. The image of that ancient, enigmatic structure the ROV had captured before the feed went dark was etched vividly in her mind. The intricate symbols, the imposing architecture it was unlike anything she had ever encountered in her years of oceanographic exploration.

"What are you?" she whispered to the sea, as if expecting an answer from the depths below.

The soft thud of approaching footsteps pulled her from her reverie. She turned to see Tommy, his youthful face etched with concern, approaching her cautiously. His usually bright and eager eyes were clouded with uncertainty, and his tousled brown hair was damp, likely from an early morning shower intended to wash away the previous day's stress.

"Morning, Dr. Hartley," he greeted, offering a tentative smile that didn't quite reach his eyes.

"Morning, Tommy," Evelyn replied, forcing a semblance of warmth into her voice. She gestured toward the mug in her hands. "Coffee?"

He nodded gratefully, accepting the spare mug she produced from a nearby table. As he poured himself a cup from the insulated carafe, Evelyn studied him closely. Tommy was one of the youngest members of the team, fresh-faced and full of ambition. But today, he seemed older, the weight of their mission pressing down on his slender shoulders.

They stood in companionable silence for a few moments, each lost in their thoughts as the sea murmured softly around them.

"Couldn't sleep either?" Tommy finally broke the silence, his voice barely above a whisper.

Evelyn shook her head, exhaling a weary sigh. "Too much on my mind, I suppose. You?"

"Same here," he admitted, wrapping his hands around the warm mug as if seeking comfort. "I kept seeing that structure every time I closed my eyes. It was... unsettling."

"Unsettling is one word for it," Evelyn agreed, her gaze drifting back toward the horizon. "Fascinating, mysterious, terrifying all apply."

Tommy hesitated before speaking again, his voice tinged with apprehension. "Do you think we should go back? Try to retrieve the ROV? Maybe get a closer look?"

Evelyn considered his question, weighing the risks and benefits carefully. The thought had crossed her mind multiple times throughout the restless night. Part of her was desperate to return, to uncover the secrets that lay hidden beneath the waves. But another part, a more cautious voice that she rarely heeded, warned of dangers they couldn't comprehend.

"I don't know, Tommy," she replied honestly. "We barely made it out of there last night, and the equipment failures, the storm... It's as if something doesn't want us there."

He nodded slowly, digesting her words. "But isn't that all the more reason to go back? To find out what it is. Maybe even understand what happened to Flight 753?"

Evelyn turned to face him fully, seeing the earnest determination in his eyes. Despite his youth, Tommy possessed a courage and curiosity that reminded her of herself at his age. It was both inspiring and concerning.

"You're right," she conceded, offering a small, tired smile. "But we need to be smart about it. We can't rush in blind, not after what happened."

Tommy's face brightened slightly at her words. "Maybe we can recalibrate some of the other equipment, strengthen the signal outputs. I could work with the engineering team to modify one of the spare drones for deep-sea exploration."

Evelyn raised an eyebrow, impressed by his initiative. "That's ambitious. Do you think it's possible?"

He took a sip of his coffee, nodding with more confidence. "It won't be as advanced as the ROV we lost, but it could get us some visual data at least. Better than going in empty-handed."

She pondered his suggestion, the gears in her mind beginning to turn anew. Perhaps all was not lost after all. With some ingenuity and teamwork, they might still salvage this mission.

"Alright," she agreed, her voice firming with renewed purpose. "Let's put together a meeting with the engineering and science teams. We'll discuss our options and come up with a plan."

Tommy's smile widened, a spark of excitement igniting in his eyes. "Yes, ma'am. I'll get right on it."

As he turned to leave, Evelyn called after him, "And Tommy?"

He glanced back, hopeful.

"Good work. Your initiative is appreciated."

He ducked his head modestly, the tips of his ears turning pink. "Just doing my part, Doctor."

As he disappeared into the maze of corridors leading below deck, Evelyn allowed herself a moment of optimism. The despair that had threatened to consume her was slowly giving way to determination. They had faced setbacks before, and they had always found a way to adapt and overcome.

She took another sip of her coffee, savouring the warmth that spread through her chest. The mist was beginning to lift, revealing streaks of pale blue sky above. Perhaps it was a sign that today would bring better fortune.

"Back to the drawing board," she murmured to herself, draining the last of her coffee before heading toward the bridge to consult with Captain Harris.

The bridge of the Nautilus was a hive of subdued activity. The crew moved with practiced efficiency, their faces etched with concentration as they monitored the ship's systems and navigational equipment. The space was filled with the soft hum of electronics and the occasional crackle of radio static, creating a backdrop of white noise that was oddly comforting.

Captain Harris stood at the centre; his broad frame silhouetted against the large panoramic windows that offered a sweeping view of the ocean ahead. His weathered face was set in a thoughtful frown, eyes narrowed as he studied the horizon. The lines around his eyes and mouth seemed deeper today, the toll of recent events evident in his posture.

"Captain," Evelyn greeted as she stepped onto the bridge, her boots clicking softly against the polished floor.

Harris turned to face her, his stern expression softening slightly. "Dr. Hartley. You're up early."

"Couldn't sleep," she replied, offering a brief smile. "Thought I'd get a head start on figuring out our next move." He nodded, gesturing for her to join him by the navigation console. "I've been mulling over the same thing. Last night was... rough."

"That's putting it mildly," Evelyn agreed, her gaze flickering to the digital displays that lined the console. "Any new developments?"

Harris sighed, running a hand through his greying hair. "Weather reports are favourable for the next 48 hours. Sea conditions are stable. But our equipment took a beating during the storm. Comms are spotty, and some of our navigational systems are acting up."

Evelyn frowned, concern creasing her brow. "I thought the storm had passed. Why are the systems still malfunctioning?"

"That's the strange part," Harris replied, his voice lowering conspiratorially. "Our engineers have been running diagnostics all morning. No mechanical faults detected. It's as if there's some kind of external interference disrupting our instruments."

A chill ran down Evelyn's spine at his words. She recalled the erratic readings and equipment failures they had experienced near the site where they lost the ROV. Could the same mysterious force be affecting them even now, miles away from that cursed location?

"Electromagnetic interference?" she speculated, trying to keep her voice steady.

"Possibly," Harris acknowledged, his eyes darkening. "But the source is unclear. We're in open waters, far from any natural or man-made disturbances that could cause this level of disruption."

Evelyn bit her lower lip thoughtfully, her mind racing. "Could it be connected to the anomaly we detected near the structure? Maybe its influence extends farther than we realized."

Harris's gaze met hers, and for a moment, unspoken understanding passed between them. Despite their diverse backgrounds she is a scientist, he a seasoned sailor, they both sensed that they were dealing with something beyond the ordinary.

"It's a possibility we can't ignore," Harris admitted, his voice grave. "Which raises the question`` do we proceed or cut our losses and head back to port?"

Evelyn's instinctive response was immediate. "We proceed."

Harris arched an eyebrow, a hint of scepticism in his eyes. "Even with the risks involved. We:ve already lost valuable equipment, and our systems are compromised. Not to mention the safety of the crew."

She took a deep breath, choosing her words carefully. "I understand the risks, Captain, and I don't take them lightly. But think about what we found or almost found. That structure could be the key to understanding not just the disappearance of Flight 753, but perhaps many other mysteries associated with this region."

She paused, her eyes shining with conviction. "If we turn back now, we may never get another opportunity like this. We owe it to ourselves, to science, and to the families of those who were lost to find the answers."

Harris studied her intently, his expression unreadable. After a long moment, he sighed deeply, nodding in resignation. "You're a stubborn one, Dr. Hartley. But perhaps that's exactly what's needed here."

A small smile tugged at the corners of Evelyn's mouth. "So, you'll support continuing the mission?"

"I will," he confirmed, his tone firm. "But on one condition."

"Name it."

"We prioritize the safety of everyone on board. The moment I feel the risks outweigh the potential gains; we pull back. Agreed?"

"Agreed," Evelyn said without hesitation, relief flooding through her.

Harris extended his hand, and she clasped it firmly, sealing their agreement. "I'll have my crew coordinate with yours to assess and repair our systems as best we can. And I'll set a course back to the coordinates we left last night."

"Thank you, Captain," she replied earnestly. "I appreciate your support."

He released her hand, a glimmer of wry humour returning to his eyes. "Just make sure this discovery of yours is worth all the trouble, Doctor."

Evelyn chuckled softly, some of the tension easing from her shoulders. "I'll do my best."

As she left the bridge, a sense of purpose invigorated her steps. There was much to do and little time to waste. She needed to assemble her team, formulate a plan, and prepare for whatever awaited them beneath the waves.

But despite the challenges ahead, Evelyn felt a spark of excitement reignite within her. The unknown beckoned, and she was ready to answer its call.

The ship's main conference room buzzed with activity as members of the science and engineering teams filtered in, taking their seats around the large oval table that dominated the space. Charts, schematics, and photographs were spread out across the table's surface, alongside steaming cups of coffee and hastily scribbled notes.

Evelyn stood at the head of the table, her presence commanding yet approachable. She had exchanged her earlier casual attire for a crisp white lab coat, the pockets bulging with pens, notebooks, and various instruments. Her hair was neatly tied back, and her eyes sparkled with focus and determination.

Tommy sat to her right, a tablet in hand as he reviewed the modifications he had proposed for the spare drone. Across from him sat Dr. Marcus Langford, the Nautilus's chief engineer'a tall, stoic man with sharp features and a keen intellect. Around them, a dozen other team members conversed in hushed tones, their expressions a mix of curiosity and trepidation.

Evelyn cleared her throat, immediately capturing the room's attention. The murmurs subsided, and all eyes turned toward her.

"Thank you all for coming on such short notice," she began, her voice clear and authoritative. "As you're all aware, last night's mission did not go as planned. We lost valuable equipment and encountered phenomena that we did not anticipate."

She paused, allowing her words to sink in before continuing. "However, we also made a significant discovery an underwater structure of unknown origin that could hold the key to understanding the disappearance of Flight 753 and perhaps much more."

A ripple of interest passed through the room, and Evelyn seized upon it, gesturing toward a projection screen that displayed the last captured image from the ROV a grainy but unmistakable view of the mysterious structure.

"This is what we saw before we lost contact with the ROV," she explained, her gaze sweeping across the faces of her colleagues. "The architecture and markings suggest a civilization or presence that we have no record of. This is an unprecedented opportunity for discovery."

Dr. Langford leaned forward; his brow furrowed. "What about the electromagnetic interference? Our instruments were severely disrupted near that location. It poses a significant risk to any further exploration."

Evelyn nodded, acknowledging his concern. "You're correct, Marcus. The interference is a serious issue. That's why we're here to discuss how we can adapt and overcome these challenges."

Tommy spoke up, his youthful enthusiasm evident despite the gravity of the situation. "I've been working on retrofitting one of our spare drones with enhanced shielding and signal boosters. It won't be as capable as the ROV, but it should withstand the interference long enough to get us some data."

Langford regarded him skeptically. "That drone wasn't designed for deep-sea exploration. Modifying it adequately would take time and resources we may not have."

"True," Tommy conceded, undeterred. "But if we all pitch in, we can expedite the process. It's our best shot at getting back down there without exposing the crew to unnecessary danger."

A murmur of agreement rose from several team members, and Evelyn smiled appreciatively at Tommy before addressing Langford. "Marcus, can your team assist with the modifications? We need all hands-on deck."

The engineer considered for a moment before nodding decisively. "We'll do what we can. But I still recommend caution. We don't fully understand what we're dealing with down there."

"Agreed," Evelyn affirmed, her tone serious. "This mission will proceed with the utmost care. We'll establish safety protocols and contingency plans. Our priority is to gather information while ensuring the well-being of everyone involved."

A hand shot up from further down the table, belonging to Dr. Sarah Patel, a marine biologist with extensive experience in deep-sea ecosystems. Her dark eyes were alight with curiosity as she spoke.

"Do we have any theories about the structure's origin? Could it be a natural formation, or are we looking at evidence of an unknown civilization?"

Evelyn exchanged a glance with Tommy before replying. "At this point, all possibilities are on the table. The structure's design and markings don't match any known geological or man-made formations. That's why it's crucial we gather more data."

Another voice chimed in, this time from Lieutenant Mark Davis, the ship's security officer. His stern demeanor added gravity to his words. "What about the potential risks? We encountered unknown forces last night. How can we be sure we won't face worse this time?"

Evelyn met his gaze steadily. "We can't be certain. But by enhancing our equipment and proceeding with caution, we can mitigate many of the risks. We'll monitor all systems closely and be prepared to abort the mission at the first sign of danger."

Davis nodded, though his expression remained cautious. "Understood. I'll coordinate with my team to ensure all safety measures are in place."

"Thank you, Lieutenant," Evelyn replied gratefully.

She took a moment to survey the room, gauging the mood. The initial apprehension seemed to be giving way to a collective resolve, a shared desire to confront the unknown despite the inherent risks.

"Any further questions or suggestions?" she prompted.

When none were forthcoming, she concluded the meeting. "Alright then. Let's get to work. Time is of the essence, and we've got a lot to do."

Chairs scraped against the floor as team members rose, conversations resuming as they discussed tasks and plans. Evelyn felt a surge of pride and affection for her crew their courage and dedication were unwavering, even in the face of daunting challenges.

As the room emptied, Tommy lingered behind, gathering his notes and tablet. Evelyn approached him, placing a reassuring hand on his shoulder.

"Good job today, Tommy. Your ideas are invaluable."

He looked up, his face flushing slightly with pleasure. "Thanks, Dr. Hartley. I'm just glad to help."

She smiled warmly. "—eep up the good work. We'll need your enthusiasm and skills more than ever in the days to come."

He nodded earnestly before heading out to join the engineering team.

Left alone in the now-quiet conference room, Evelyn allowed herself a moment to collect her thoughts. The path ahead was fraught with uncertainty, but they were making progress. With a solid plan and a committed team, perhaps they could unravel the mysteries that awaited them beneath the ocean's depths.

As she exited the room and made her way toward the lab, she couldn't shake the feeling that they were standing on the precipice of a discovery that would change everything they thought they knew about the world and perhaps even about themselves.

Little did she know, the secrets lurking below were far more profound and perilous than any of them could imagine.

Chapter 3

The midday sun had climbed high into the sky, burning away the last remnants of the morning mist. The Nautilus hummed with renewed purpose as the crew busied themselves with the preparations for the next dive. The ship had become a hive of activity, with voices echoing through the steel corridors and footsteps pounding rhythmically against the metal floors.

Evelyn moved through the ship with a sense of focused determination, her mind a whirl of calculations and plans. She had just left the engineering bay, where Dr. Langford and his team were deep into the modifications of the spare drone. They had stripped the device down to its core components, and Tommy was leading the effort to enhance its capabilities. Despite the challenges, the team's progress was impressive, and they hoped to have the drone operational by the evening.

As she made her way toward the lab, Evelyn couldn't help but replay the meeting in her mind. The enthusiasm and resolve of her team were encouraging, but she was acutely aware of the risks they were taking. The mysteries they were venturing to uncover were layered with dangers, dangers that might not even be fully comprehensible.

The lab was a sanctuary of science, a place where Evelyn could lose herself in the comforting logic of data and hypotheses. The room was filled with state-of-the-art equipment microscopes, spectrometers, and computers with massive processing power all humming with energy. The walls were lined with whiteboards covered in equations, notes, and hastily drawn diagrams, all evidence of the team's relentless pursuit of understanding.

Evelyn entered the lab to find Dr. Sarah Patel and Dr. Carlos Ramirez, the team's marine geologist, engrossed in a discussion over a digital projection of the seafloor. The image displayed the area surrounding the mysterious structure they had briefly glimpsed through the ROV before losing it.

Carlos, a tall man with salt-and-pepper hair and a perpetual five o'clock shadow, was pointing at a series of unusual formations on the map. His deep voice resonated with the authority of someone who had spent years studying the Earth's crust.

"Look at these ridges," he was saying as Evelyn approached. "They're not natural. They run in a pattern that suggests deliberate design almost like a foundation."

"Foundation for what?" Evelyn asked, stepping up to the table and scrutinizing the projection.

Carlos glanced at her; his dark eyes intense. "That's the question, isn't it? Whatever this structure is, it's ancient. The geological layers surrounding it indicate that it's been here for millennia possibly tens of thousands of years."

Sarah nodded; her expression thoughtful as she manipulated the controls to zoom in on a particular section. "The way these formations are laid out... it's almost like a city or a complex of buildings. But that doesn't make any sense. If a civilization existed at those depths, we would have found evidence of it before."

"Unless," Carlos added, his voice dropping to a near whisper, "it's been hidden from us. Buried by time or some other force."

Evelyn felt a shiver run down her spine at his words. The thought that an entire civilization could exist, concealed beneath the ocean's depths, was both thrilling and terrifying. What kind of beings could have built such a structure? And why had it been forgotten or hidden from the world?

"What about the markings on the structure?" Evelyn asked, trying to steer the conversation back to the evidence they had. "Do we have any leads on what they could mean?" Sarah hesitated, clearly uncertain. "I've run the images through every database we have access to. None of the symbols match any known language or script. But there's something about them… a pattern, maybe. I can't quite put my finger on it."

Evelyn's mind raced; her scientific curiosity piqued. "Can we enhance the images? Maybe run them through a different set of filters to see if we can pull out more detail?"

"We can try," Sarah replied, already pulling up the necessary software. "It's a long shot, but worth it."

As Sarah began the process of analyzing the images, Evelyn turned to Carlos. "What about the surrounding environment? Is there anything unusual about the area around the structure?"

Carlos frowned, tapping a few keys on his tablet to bring up a series of environmental readings. "The area has elevated levels of electromagnetic activity similar to what we experienced during the storm. It's localized, though, concentrated around the structure itself. There are also fluctuations in temperature and pressure that don't align with normal oceanic patterns."

"Could that explain the interference we've been experiencing?" Evelyn asked, her brow furrowing.

"It's possible," Carlos conceded. "But there's something else something I can't quite explain. The readings we're getting… they're almost as if the area is alive, reacting to our presence."

Evelyn's heart skipped a beat at his words. "Alive?"

"Not in the biological sense," Carlos clarified quickly. "More like... the environment is dynamic, shifting in response to external stimuli. It's like nothing I've ever seen before."

Evelyn considered his words carefully. The Bermuda Triangle had long been associated with mysterious phenomena ships and planes disappearing without a trace, unexplained electromagnetic disturbances, and strange lights in the sky. Could all these events be connected to this ancient structure? Was it possible that they had stumbled upon the source of the Triangle's infamous reputation?

A knock at the door interrupted her thoughts, and she turned to see Lieutenant Mark Davis standing in the doorway. The security officer's face was grim, his posture rigid with tension.

"Evelyn," he said, his voice clipped, "we need to talk."

She felt a knot of apprehension form in her stomach. "What is it, Mark?"

"There's been an incident on deck," he replied, his tone brooking no argument. "You should come with me."

Evelyn exchanged a quick glance with Sarah and Carlos, who both looked equally concerned. "I'll be right back," she told them before following Mark out of the lab.

The atmosphere on deck was thick with tension as Evelyn and Mark emerged into the open air. The crew members moved with an undercurrent of anxiety, their eyes darting nervously as they spoke in hushed tones. It was clear that whatever had happened had shaken them deeply.

Mark led Evelyn toward the starboard side, where a small group had gathered around a prone figure lying on the deck. As they approached, Evelyn recognized the figure as Ensign Hannah Mills, one of the ship's communications officers.

Hannah was conscious but pale, her breathing shallow and rapid. She was being attended to by Dr. Lila Morgan, the ship's medical officer, who looked up with a worried expression as Evelyn and Mark arrived.

"What happened?" Evelyn asked, dropping to her knees beside Hannah.

Dr. Morgan shook her head, her face etched with concern. "She collapsed about ten minutes ago. Said she felt dizzy and then just... went down. I've checked her vitals—they're stable, but she's disoriented and weak."

Hannah's eyes fluttered open, and she tried to sit up, wincing as she did so. "I'm fine," she insisted weakly, though her voice betrayed her fragility. "Just a little lightheaded."

"You need to rest," Dr. Morgan said firmly, placing a hand on Hannah's shoulder to keep her from moving too much.
"I'll take you to the infirmary and run some tests."

Evelyn leaned closer; her voice gentle but probing. "Hannah, can you tell us what happened before you collapsed? Did you feel anything unusual?"

Hannah blinked, her brow furrowing as she tried to recall. "I was... I was checking the comms systems. There was interference, so I went to adjust the settings. And then... I don't know. It was like everything went fuzzy. My head started spinning, and I felt this pressure in my chest."

"Pressure?" Evelyn echoed, her mind racing to connect the dots. "Was it liking the pressure you feel when you're diving, or something different?"

"Different," Hannah replied, her voice faint. "It was... internal. Like something was pushing against me from the inside."

Evelyn exchanged a troubled glance with Mark. The description was eerily like the symptoms of decompression sickness, but they were on the surface Hannah hadn't been diving. Could the electromagnetic interference be affecting the crew physically? Or was there something more insidious at work?

"Let's get you to the infirmary," Evelyn said softly, helping Dr. Morgan lift Hannah to her feet. "We'll run some tests and figure this out."

As they escorted Hannah below deck, Evelyn couldn't shake the feeling that they were venturing into territory far more dangerous than they had anticipated. The mysterious structure below was not just a relic of the past it was a force, a presence that seemed to reach out and touch those who dared to come near.

The infirmary was a small but well-equipped space, its white walls and sterile surfaces designed to instil a sense of calm and order. Dr. Morgan guided Hannah to one of the examination beds and began preparing to run a series of tests. Evelyn stood nearby, her mind churning with questions.

As Dr. Morgan worked, Evelyn's thoughts drifted to the other strange occurrences that had plagued their mission the electromagnetic interference, the storm that had appeared out of nowhere, and now Hannah's mysterious collapse. It was as if the deeper they delved into the Bermuda Triangle's secrets, the more it pushed back, resisting their efforts to uncover the truth.

"What do you think caused this, Lila?" Evelyn asked, breaking the silence.

Dr. Morgan glanced at her, her expression troubled. "I'm not sure. Hannah's symptoms don't match anything I've seen before. It's almost like her body was reacting to some external force, but I can't pinpoint what that force might be."

"Could it be related to the structure we found?" Evelyn suggested. "The electromagnetic readings we've been getting are off the charts. Maybe it's affecting the crew in ways we don't fully understand."

"It's possible," Dr. Morgan conceded, though she didn't sound entirely convinced. "But electromagnetic fields shouldn't cause these kinds of physical symptoms not at the levels we've recorded. Unless..." Her voice trailed off as she considered the implications.

"Unless what?" Evelyn prompted.

"Unless there's something else at play something we haven't detected yet," Dr. Morgan finished, her eyes dark with worry.

Evelyn nodded slowly, her mind working through the possibilities. If there was an unknown force emanating from the structure, it could be affecting the entire ship and crew in ways they hadn't anticipated. And if that was the case, they needed to figure out how to protect themselves fast.

As Dr. Morgan continued her examination, Evelyn's thoughts were interrupted by the sudden sound of the ship's alarm system blaring to life. The shrill noise echoed through the infirmary, sending a jolt of adrenaline through her veins.

"What now?" Dr. Morgan muttered, her hands pausing mid-motion.

Evelyn didn't wait to find out. She turned and bolted out of the infirmary, racing toward the source of the alarm. Whatever was happening, it was clear that their mission was becoming more dangerous by the minute.

By the time Evelyn reached the bridge, the ship was in chaos. The storm that had appeared on the horizon earlier had intensified rapidly, its dark clouds swirling overhead like a malevolent vortex. The wind howled through the rigging, and the sea had transformed into a churning mass of whitecaps, crashing against the hull with relentless fury.

Harris was at the helm, barking orders to the crew as they struggled to keep the Nautilus on course. His usual calm demeanor was gone, replaced by a look of grim determination as he fought against the elements.

"Evelyn!" he called out as she entered the bridge. "We've lost contact with the drones, and the storm's getting worse by the minute. I'm not sure how much longer we can hold our position."

"What caused the alarm?" Evelyn asked, grabbing onto the nearest console to steady herself as the ship rocked violently.

"Something's happening below us," Harris replied, his voice tense. "The structure it's emitting some kind of energy pulse. It's affecting our systems navigation, communications, everything."

Evelyn's heart raced as she processed his words. If the structure was indeed emitting energy, it could be the source of the storm, or at the very least, amplifying it. And if they didn't figure out how to counteract it, the Nautilus could be in serious trouble.

"We need to get to the bottom of this," she said urgently. "We need to send the modified drone down now, while we still have a chance."

Harris hesitated, his eyes flicking to the storm outside. "Are you sure it's ready? If we lose the drone...."

"It's a risk we have to take," Evelyn interrupted, her voice firm. "We need answers, and the drone is our best shot at getting them. We have to understand what we're dealing with before it's too late."

Captain Harris nodded, his expression resolute. "Do it."

Evelyn wasted no time. She sprinted to the communications console and relayed the order to Tommy and Dr. Langford. The team was ready, and within minutes, the modified drone was being deployed into the water, its sensors and cameras calibrated to withstand the intense conditions.

As the drone descended into the depths, Evelyn and the crew watched the live feed with bated breath. The screen flickered and distorted as the interference grew stronger, but the drone pressed on, its mechanical arms reaching out to navigate the treacherous terrain.

Finally, the drone's camera locked onto the structure. The image was blurry and filled with static, but it was clear enough to see that the structure was pulsating with energy, its surface glowing with an eerie, otherworldly light.

"What is that?" someone muttered, their voice filled with awe and fear.

Evelyn didn't answer. She was too focused on the readings coming from the drone electromagnetic spikes, temperature fluctuations, and a strange, rhythmic vibration that seemed to resonate through the water.

And then, without warning, the structure began to change. The pulsating light intensified, and the energy readings skyrocketed. The drone's camera captured the moment as the structure seemed to come alive, its surface shifting and transforming before their eyes.

A low hum filled the air, growing louder and more intense until it felt like the very air was vibrating. The crew exchanged nervous glances; the fear palpable in the room.

Evelyn's eyes were locked on the screen, her mind racing to comprehend what she was seeing. The structure was not just a relic of the past it was active, powerful, and possibly sentient. And whatever it was doing, it was about to reach its climax.

"Brace yourselves!" Harris shouted, his voice cutting through the tension like a knife.

And then, in a flash of blinding light, the world around them exploded into chaos.

Chapter 4

The world dissolved into a blinding white light, a surge of energy that seemed to penetrate through the very atoms of Evelyn's being. She had only a fraction of a second to process what was happening a mixture of awe, terror, and scientific curiosity flashing through her mind before everything went dark.

She didn't know how long she remained in that void, suspended between consciousness and oblivion. Time felt meaningless, as if she were adrift in an endless sea, her thoughts scattered like debris after a storm.

Gradually, Evelyn became aware of herself again first as a distant, floating awareness, then as a being with a body, a mind, and memories. Her senses returned in fragments: the soft hum of machinery, the distant echo of voices, the sharp tang of antiseptic in the air.

When she finally opened her eyes, the world around her was blurred and unfocused. She blinked, struggling to bring her surroundings into clarity. Slowly, the room began to take shape a small, sterile chamber bathed in dim light. She was lying on a narrow cot, a thin blanket draped over her, and as she shifted, she realized that every muscle in her body ached as though she had been through a battle.

Evelyn's world was nothing but light and sound, a cacophony that obliterated all sense of time and space. The blinding flash from the mysterious structure seemed to have fused with her consciousness, dragging her into an abyss where reality fractured into a thousand disjointed pieces.

When the light finally receded, it left behind a haunting silence. Evelyn struggled to gather her thoughts, but they felt like sand slipping through her fingers. Her body felt weightless, her limbs unresponsive as if she were floating in a void. Was she still on the Nautilus? Was she even alive?

Slowly, as though fighting through a thick fog, she began to regain some semblance of awareness. Her senses returned in fragments first the cold metal floor beneath her, then the distant sound of groaning steel as the ship strained against the storm. The dull throb of pain pulsed at the back of her head, and she realized she was lying sprawled across the bridge floor, her body still recovering from the shock.

Her eyes fluttered open, blinking against the remnants of the searing light that had overwhelmed them. The world swam back into focus, and she saw the bridge around her wrecked, chaotic, and filled with the groans and muffled voices of her crew mates.

Evelyn forced herself to sit up, her movements sluggish as if her muscles had forgotten how to function. Every nerve in her body screamed in protest, but she gritted her teeth and pushed through the pain. She had to assess the situation, understand what had just happened.

The bridge was in shambles. Consoles flickered with distorted images or were completely dark, their screens shattered by the force of the blast. Several of the overhead panels had been ripped from the ceiling, exposing a tangle of wires that sparked and sputtered like wounded serpents. The air was thick with the acrid scent of burning electronics and the metallic tang of blood.

Her heart lurched when she saw Captain Harris slumped against the helm, his hand pressed to a gash on his forehead that was bleeding profusely. His face was pale, but his eyes were sharp with determination as he tried to regain control of the ship's failing systems.

"Captain!" Evelyn's voice was hoarse, her throat dry and raw from the scream that had been ripped from her during the blast. She scrambled to her feet, swaying unsteadily as the ship listed beneath her.

Harris looked up, his eyes locking onto hers. Relief flickered across his features. "Evelyn," he rasped, wincing as he straightened. "Thank God you're okay."

She reached his side, her hands shaking as she tried to help him stem the bleeding. "What happened? The structure did it… did it attack us?"

Harris grimaced, his grip tightening on the helm as the ship lurched again. "I don't know. One moment we were watching it, the next… everything went to hell. It's like it released some kind of energy pulse, but I've never seen anything like it."

Evelyn's mind spun, trying to process his words. An energy pulse that explained the overwhelming light and the chaos that had followed. But why? What had triggered the structure to unleash such power?

A groan from behind them drew her attention, and she turned to see Sarah Patel lying amidst a pile of debris, her face twisted in pain as she tried to move. Without thinking, Evelyn rushed to her side, dropping to her knees beside the scientist.

"Sarah, don't move," she said quickly, her hands hovering over Sarah's prone form. "You might be injured."

Sarah's eyes fluttered open, and she let out a shaky breath. "I'm okay… I think. Just… a little bruised." She winced as she tried to sit up, clutching her side where a large bruise was already forming.

"Take it slow," Evelyn urged, helping her into a sitting position. "We've been through some kind of shockwave. We need to check for injuries."

Sarah nodded; her expression dazed as she surveyed the wreckage around them. "What… what was that? It felt like we were hit by a bomb."

"I don't know," Evelyn admitted, her voice barely above a whisper. "But we need to get the ship stabilized and assess the damage."

As if on cue, the ship shuddered violently, the storm outside still raging with unchecked fury. The waves crashed against the hull with enough force to rattle the entire structure, and the wind howled like a living creature, its fury unrelenting.

"We need to get to engineering," Sarah said, her voice growing stronger as she regained her composure. "If the pulse damaged the systems, we could be dead in the water."

Evelyn nodded, helping Sarah to her feet. "Let's move. We need to check on the rest of the crew, too."

The two women made their way through the bridge, helping other crew members who were slowly regaining consciousness. Dr. Langford was propped against a console, his face pale and drawn but conscious. Carlos Ramirez was sitting on the floor, his hands trembling as he tried to steady his breathing. Lieutenant Mark Davis was already on his feet, barking orders to the remaining crew to assess the damage.

Despite the chaos, Evelyn felt a strange sense of clarity settle over her. The fear and confusion that had gripped her were giving way to a cold, determined resolve. Whatever had happened, they were still alive. And as long as they were alive, they could fight to understand the forces they were dealing with.

With the bridge somewhat stabilized, Evelyn and Sarah made their way down to the lower decks, where the engineering bay was located. The corridors were dimly lit, the emergency lights casting an eerie red glow that made everything look surreal, as though they were walking through a nightmare.

The air was thick with tension, the silence broken only by the distant sounds of the storm and the occasional groan of the ship's hull as it strained against the waves. Evelyn's heart pounded in her chest, each step echoing loudly in her ears as she tried to push aside the gnawing fear that something was terribly, irreversibly wrong.

They passed by the infirmary, where Dr. Lila Morgan was still tending to Hannah Mills. The young ensign was awake but weak, her face pale as she lay on the examination bed. Lila glanced up as Evelyn and Sarah passed, giving them a brief nod of acknowledgement before returning to her work.

Evelyn couldn't help but feel a pang of guilt as she continued down the corridor. Hannah had collapsed before the pulse, and now this was it all connected? Had they triggered something that was beyond their understanding?

When they finally reached the engineering bay, they found Tommy and his team working frantically to stabilize the ship's systems. The room was a flurry of activity, with sparks flying from damaged consoles and the hum of machinery filling the air. Tommy was hunched over a control panel, his face streaked with sweat and grease as he barked orders to his crew.

"Tommy!" Evelyn called out, raising her voice to be heard over the din.

He looked up, his expression a mix of relief and frustration. "Evelyn! We're barely holding it together down here. That pulse knocked out half our systems, and the backup generators are struggling to keep up."

"What about the drone?" Sarah asked, her voice urgent. "Did it survive the pulse?"

Tommy shook his head, his eyes dark with frustration. "We lost contact with it right after the blast. I'm trying to bring the systems back online to see if we can re-establish a connection, but it's not looking good."

Evelyn felt a sinking feeling in her stomach. The drone had been their best chance at understanding what had happened, and now it was lost in the depths, possibly destroyed. But she couldn't let despair take hold not yet.

"Do what you can," she said, her voice firm. "We need to get the ship stabilized and figure out what we're dealing with. If that structure is still active, we need to know."

Tommy nodded; his expression grim. "We're working on it. But it's going to take time. That pulse scrambled everything it's like the whole ship's been hit by an EMP."

Evelyn exchanged a worried glance with Sarah. An electromagnetic pulse if that's what it had been could have devastating effects on their equipment, and possibly on the crew as well. They were in uncharted waters, both literally and figuratively.

"Keep us updated," she told Tommy, turning to leave the bay. "We're going to check the rest of the ship."

As they made their way back to the upper decks, Evelyn's mind churned with questions. The structure they had discovered what was it? Why had it reacted so violently? And most importantly, what were they going to do now?

The storm outside was still raging, its fury undiminished, and she couldn't shake the feeling that it was somehow connected to the events unfolding below the surface. The Bermuda Triangle had always been a place of mystery and legend, but now she was beginning to understand just how dangerous those mysteries could be.

Back on the bridge, the atmosphere was tense as the crew worked to assess the damage and stabilize the ship. Harris had managed to regain partial control of the helm, but the ship was still being tossed about by the storm, its progress slow and uncertain.

Evelyn and Sarah returned to find the situation only slightly improved. The crew had managed to restore some of the ship's systems, but the damage was extensive, and it was clear that they were operating on borrowed time.

"Status report,"

Chapter 5

As the hours dragged on, Evelyn found herself alone in her quarters, finally allowing herself a moment to breathe. She sat on the edge of her bunk, her hands trembling as she tried to process everything that had happened.

The events of the day played out in her mind like a distorted film reel Hannah's collapse, the discovery of the structure, the pulse that had nearly destroyed them. It all felt like a waking nightmare, and she couldn't shake the feeling that they were teetering on the edge of something far more dangerous than they had ever anticipated.

She leaned forward, resting her head in her hands as a wave of exhaustion washed over her. She had always prided herself on being rational, logical, able to tackle any problem with a clear head. But this… this was something else entirely. The unknown force they had encountered defied explanation, and the more she tried to understand it, the more it eluded her grasp.

A soft knock on the door pulled her from her thoughts. She looked up to see Sarah standing in the doorway, her face etched with concern.

"Hey," Sarah said gently, stepping inside. "How are you holding up?"

Evelyn managed a weak smile. "I've been better."

Sarah sat down beside her, the two women sharing a moment of silence. The bond they had formed over the course of the mission was strong, built on mutual respect and a shared determination to see things through. But now, that bond was being tested in ways neither of them could have imagined.

"We'll get through this," Sarah said quietly, her voice filled with conviction. "We've come too far to turn back now."

Evelyn nodded, drawing strength from her friend's words. "I know. It's just… there's so much we don't understand. And I'm afraid we might be in over our heads."

Sarah's hand found hers, squeezing it reassuringly. "We're scientists, Evelyn. We've faced the unknown before. We'll find the answers, we just need to keep our heads and stick together."

Evelyn took a deep breath, letting Sarah's words settle over her like a comforting blanket. She was right. They had faced challenges before, and they had always come through.

This time would be no different.

But even as she tried to convince herself of that, a nagging doubt lingered at the back of her mind. The Bermuda Triangle was a place of legend, a place where the rules of reality seemed to bend and twist. And now, they were at its mercy.

She had to believe they would find a way out. But deep down, she couldn't shake the feeling that they had only scratched the surface of the mysteries that lay ahead.

The following hours were a blur of activity as the crew worked tirelessly to repair the damage and restore the ship's systems. The storm outside showed no signs of abating, its fury a constant reminder of the danger they were in.

Evelyn spent most of the time on the bridge, coordinating with the crew and monitoring the progress of the repairs. The atmosphere was tense, every small victory tempered by the knowledge that they were still in grave danger.

But as the night wore on, a strange calm settled over the ship. The storm, though still fierce, seemed to recede just enough to allow them a brief respite. It was as if the forces at play had withdrawn, biding their time before striking again.

Evelyn stood at the helm, gazing out at the churning sea. The water was dark and foreboding, the waves lit only by the faint glow of the ship's lights. In the distance, the clouds swirled ominously, their edges tinged with an unnatural, otherworldly light.

She couldn't shake the feeling that they were being watched that something out there something ancient and powerful was observing their every move. The thought sent a shiver down her spine, and she wrapped her arms around herself, trying to ward off the chill.

"Evelyn," Harris's voice broke through her thoughts, drawing her attention.

She turned to see him standing beside her, his expression unreadable. "Captain," she acknowledged, her voice quiet.

He studied her for a moment, his gaze intense. "We're in uncharted territory," he said finally. "Whatever that structure is, it's not something we were prepared for. But I need to know do you think we can survive this?"

Evelyn met his gaze, the weight of his question pressing down on her. She didn't have all the answers, how could she?
But she knew one thing: they couldn't afford to give up.

"We'll survive," she said, her voice steady. "We have to."

Harris nodded, his expression softening. "I'm counting on you, Evelyn. We all are."

The weight of his words settled over her, but instead of crushing her, it gave her strength. She wasn't alone in this they were all in it together. And as long as they stood united, they had a chance.

As the night stretched on, Evelyn found herself standing alone on the bridge, the quiet hum of the ship's systems a stark contrast to the storm that still raged outside. She watched as the clouds twisted and churned, their movements hypnotic and terrifying all at once.

And in that moment, she made a silent vow: no matter what lay ahead, she would see this mission through to the end. She would uncover the truth behind the Bermuda Triangle and the mysterious structure that had nearly destroyed them.

But as she gazed out at the endless expanse of water, she couldn't help but wonder: at what cost?

The answer, she feared, was something they were all about to discover.

Chapter 6

Evelyn awoke to the sound of distant thunder rolling through the ship, a deep rumble that resonated in her bones. For a moment, she lay still, disoriented, her mind grasping for a foothold in the waking world. The events of the previous day flooded back, the memories sharp and vivid: the pulse, the chaos, the wreckage. She sat up abruptly, the blanket sliding off her shoulders as she swung her legs over the edge of the bed.

Her quarters were dimly lit, the emergency lights casting a dull red glow that only deepened the shadows. The storm outside had not relented, its fury echoing through the ship in the form of creaks and groans. The Nautilus was a vessel under siege, not by any visible enemy, but by the very forces of nature or something far more sinister.

Evelyn rubbed her temples, trying to ease the pounding headache that had settled behind her eyes. Sleep had been fitful at best, plagued by strange dreams that left her more exhausted than refreshed. She had dreamt of the structure again, its pulsating light drawing her closer and closer until it filled her vision, consuming her entire being. Even now, awake and alert, she could still feel its pull, a lingering presence at the edge of her consciousness.

A sharp knock on her door pulled her from her thoughts. She hesitated, then stood and crossed the small room to open it. Sarah stood on the other side; her expression grim.

"Evelyn, you need to come to the bridge. There's something you need to see."

Evelyn's heart skipped a beat. "What is it? What's happened?"

Sarah shook her head. "It's… difficult to explain. You'll understand when you see it."

Without another word, Evelyn grabbed her jacket from the back of a chair and followed Sarah through the narrow corridors of the ship. The air was thick with tension, the silence punctuated only by the occasional burst of static from the intercom and the ever-present roar of the storm outside.

When they reached the bridge, Evelyn immediately sensed that something was wrong. The usual hustle and bustle of the crew had been replaced by a heavy, oppressive silence. Captain Harris stood at the helm, his posture rigid, his eyes fixed on the main screen. The others were gathered around, their expressions a mix of confusion and fear.

"What's going on?" Evelyn asked, stepping forward.

Harris didn't turn to look at her. His gaze remained locked on the screen as he spoke, his voice low and tense. "We've re-established partial contact with the drone."

Evelyn's eyes widened. "It's still operational? How?"

"We don't know," Sarah said quietly, stepping up beside her. "But the feed we're getting… it's not what we expected."

Evelyn's gaze shifted to the screen, where a distorted image flickered into view. At first, it was difficult to make out any detail's static marred the feed, and the camera's focus kept shifting erratically. But as the interference cleared, the image sharpened, revealing a scene that sent a chill down Evelyn's spine.

The drone was deep beneath the ocean, its lights cutting through the inky blackness. In the distance, the structure loomed, its surface still glowing with that eerie, pulsating light. But it wasn't the structure itself that drew Evelyn's attention it was what surrounded it.

Dozens, perhaps hundreds, of shadowy figures moved in the water around the structure. Their forms were indistinct, little more than silhouettes in the murky depths, but they were clearly humanoid in shape. They drifted aimlessly, their movements slow and fluid, as if they were suspended in a trance.

Evelyn felt her blood run cold. "What… what are they?"

"We don't know," Captain Harris said, his voice grim. "The drone's sensors can't get a clear reading. They're not giving off any heat signatures, no identifiable electromagnetic fields… it's like they're not even there."

"But they are there," Sarah added, her voice trembling slightly. "You can see them, plain as day. And they're all… they're all moving toward the structure."

Evelyn's mind raced, trying to make sense of what she was seeing. The figures, the structure, the strange energy pulse it was all connected, but how? What were these beings, and why were they drawn to the structure like moths to a flame?

As if sensing her thoughts, Harris spoke again. "There's more."

Evelyn turned to him, dread coiling in her stomach. "More?"

Harris nodded to one of the crew members, who pressed a few buttons on the console. The screen shifted, and a new image appeared this one even more unsettling than the last.

The drone had descended lower, closer to the ocean floor, where the light from the structure barely reached. But in the darkness, another shape had emerged, something massive and ancient, half-buried in the silt. It was a ship a shipwreck, to be precise, its hull rusted and corroded by years beneath the sea. But this was no ordinary shipwreck.

Evelyn gasped as recognition dawned. "That's… that's the

Trident."

Sarah's eyes widened. "The missing research vessel? The one that disappeared a year ago?"

Evelyn nodded numbly, her heart pounding in her chest. The Trident had been lost in the Bermuda Triangle during a routine expedition, vanishing without a trace. Search efforts had been extensive, but no sign of the ship or its crew had ever been found until now.

"It looks like it's been here for decades," Harris said, his voice barely above a whisper. "But that's impossible. The Trident disappeared only a year ago."

Evelyn stared at the screen, her mind struggling to process the implications. The ship looked ancient, its once-sturdy frame now little more than a skeletal husk. How could it have aged so drastically in such a short period? What had happened to it and more importantly, what had happened to the crew?

As the drone moved closer to the wreck, the camera caught glimpses of the inside through broken windows and gaping holes in the hull. The interior was dark, filled with debris and the remnants of equipment. But there were no signs of life, no bodies or skeletons to indicate what had become of the crew.

And then, just as the drone passed by one of the larger holes in the hull, the screen flickered, and for a moment, Evelyn saw it another figure, standing motionless inside the wreck, its eyes glowing with an unnatural light.

The image lasted only a second before the feed cut out entirely, plunging the bridge into darkness. The silence that followed was deafening.

"What the hell was that?" Lieutenant Davis muttered, breaking the spell.

No one answered. No one knew.

The few hours were a blur of frantic activity as the crew worked to restore the drone's feed and analyse the data they had gathered. But despite their best efforts, the feed remained offline, the connection severed as if by some unseen force.

Evelyn found herself pacing the bridge, her mind racing with a thousand questions. The appearance of the Trident aged and decayed was baffling enough, but the presence of those figures, those shadowy beings that defied explanation, left her deeply unsettled.

"They looked… human," Sarah said quietly, echoing Evelyn's thoughts as they stood together by the main console. "But they couldn't be, right? No one could survive down there, not like that."

Evelyn shook her head. "I don't know. Maybe they're not alive not in the way we understand. But they're connected to the structure somehow. Maybe… maybe they were once human."

Sarah's eyes widened. "You think they could be… the crew of the Trident?"

"It's possible," Evelyn said, though the idea filled her with dread. "But if that's true, then whatever's down there has the power to alter time or at least our perception of it. The Trident looks like it's been there for decades, but it's only been a year. And those figures… they might be all that's left of the crew."

The thought hung heavy in the air between them, the implications too horrifying to fully comprehend. If the structure had the power to warp time, to transform living beings into those ghostly figures, then they were dealing with something far beyond their understanding something ancient and dangerous.

"I don't want to believe it," Sarah admitted, her voice trembling. "But after everything we've seen… how can we deny it?"

Evelyn placed a reassuring hand on her shoulder. "We'll figure this out. We have to. But we need more information more data. The drone was our best shot, but now…"

Before she could finish her sentence, the lights on the bridge flickered, and a wave of nausea washed over her. She staggered, gripping the edge of the console for support as her vision blurred and a strange, disorienting sensation swept through her.

"Evelyn?" Sarah's voice sounded distant, distorted. "Are you okay?"

But Evelyn couldn't answer. The world around her was spinning, the sounds of the bridge fading into an indistinct hum. And then, just as suddenly as it had begun, the sensation passed, leaving her breathless and shaken.

"What… what was that?" she gasped, struggling to regain her composure.

Sarah was by her side in an instant, her face pale with worry. "I don't know. You just…"

Before she could finish, the intercom crackled to life, and Captain Harris's voice came through, tense and urgent. "All crew to the bridge immediately. We've detected a massive energy surge from the structure. It's… it's moving."

Evelyn's heart skipped a beat. The structure moving? It seemed impossible, but after everything they had witnessed, she no longer trusted her own perceptions.

"We need to get up there," Evelyn said, straightening up despite the lingering dizziness. "Now."

The two women hurried through the corridors, the ship's alarms now blaring, a shrill reminder of the danger they were in. As they reached the bridge, the atmosphere was one of controlled panic. The crew was at their stations, working frantically to make sense of the readings coming in.

"What's happening?" Evelyn demanded as she entered the room.

Harris pointed to the screen, where a new image had replaced the static. The structure was there, its light now pulsing rapidly, the rhythm almost like a heartbeat. But what caught Evelyn's attention was the water around it churning, swirling, as if being drawn into a vortex.

"It's creating some kind of… energy field," Lieutenant Davis reported, his voice strained. "The readings are off the charts. Whatever it is, it's affecting everything around it the water, the currents, even the ship's systems."

"We need to get out of here," Sarah said, fear lacing her words. "If that thing can move, there's no telling what it might do."

Evelyn nodded, her mind racing. "We must understand it figure out how it works. But you're right, we can't stay here. We need to put some distance between us and that structure until we know more."

Captain Harris didn't hesitate. "Helm, full reverse. Get us clear of that field."

The ship lurched as the engines roared to life, the Nautilus straining against the pull of the energy field. The crew watched in tense silence as the distance between them and the structure slowly increased, the vortex growing smaller and smaller on the screen.

But just as it seemed they were out of danger, the lights flickered again, and the ship was rocked by a violent jolt that sent everyone sprawling to the floor.

"Damage report!" Captain Harris shouted as he scrambled to his feet.

"Engine failure!" someone called out. "We're dead in the water!"

Evelyn's heart raced as she pushed herself up, the cold dread of realization washing over her. They were trapped, caught in the grip of something beyond their understanding, and now, without power, they were completely vulnerable.

The structure's light flared on the screen, growing brighter and brighter, until it was the only thing visible a blinding beacon in the darkness.

And then, with a final, blinding flash, everything went black.

Chapter 7

Evelyn's consciousness drifted in a void of darkness. For a moment, she wasn't sure if she was awake or still dreaming, the boundary between reality and imagination blurred by the disorienting events of the past few days. The last thing she remembered was the ship being engulfed in a blinding light, a force so powerful it seemed to tear at the very fabric of her being. Now, she felt weightless, suspended in an empty space where time had no meaning.

Gradually, sensations began to return first, the cold, biting into her skin like a thousand needles. Then, the sound of her own breathing, shallow and uneven, filling the silence. And finally, the dull ache in her head, pulsing in time with her heartbeat, reminding her that she was still alive.

She forced her eyes open, blinking against the darkness. Her surroundings were dimly lit by emergency lights, casting long shadows that seemed to stretch endlessly in every direction. She was lying on the cold metal floor of the bridge, the familiar hum of the ship's systems conspicuously absent. The silence was deafening, broken only by the occasional creak of the hull as the Nautilus swayed gently in the water.

Panic flared in her chest as she scrambled to her feet, her movements unsteady. "Sarah?" she called out, her voice hoarse. "Captain Harris?"

There was no immediate response. The bridge was in disarray, consoles flickering with intermittent power, and the few screens still active displaying nothing but static. She spotted several crew members lying motionless on the floor, and her heart skipped a beat. Were they…?

"Sarah!" Evelyn shouted, louder this time, her voice echoing in the confined space.

A groan from nearby drew her attention, and she rushed over to find Sarah slowly pushing herself up from the floor, her hand pressed to the side of her head where a thin trickle of blood ran down her temple.

"Evelyn…" Sarah's voice was weak, but it was enough to send a wave of relief washing over Evelyn.

"Are you okay?" Evelyn knelt beside her, helping her to sit up. "What happened? Are you hurt?"

Sarah winced but shook her head. "I'm… I'm okay, I think. Just a little banged up. What about you?"

"I'm fine," Evelyn said quickly, though she wasn't entirely sure it was true. The pounding in her head had dulled, but the disorientation lingered, making it difficult to focus.

"What about the others?" Sarah asked, her gaze shifting to the motionless bodies of the crew members scattered around the bridge.

Evelyn followed her gaze, dread tightening in her chest. "I don't know. We need to check on them and make sure they're still alive."

Together, they moved from person to person, checking for signs of life. To their immense relief, most of the crew members were merely unconscious, likely knocked out by the same force that had thrown Evelyn and Sarah to the floor. A few of them had minor injuries bruises, cuts, and in one case, a dislocated shoulder but nothing life-threatening.

Captain Harris was the last person they found, slumped against the helm with a deep gash on his forehead. Evelyn's heart skipped a beat when she saw the blood, but he was breathing steadily, and after a few moments, he stirred, groaning as he came to.

"Captain!" Evelyn exclaimed, kneeling beside him. "Are you okay?"

His eyes fluttered open, and he looked up at her, his expression dazed. "Evelyn… what the hell happened?"

"We're not sure," Sarah answered as she joined them. "There was a surge from the structure, and then… the ship was hit by something. We lost power, and…"

Harris shook his head, wincing as he did so. "I remember the flash. It felt like the whole ship was being torn apart."

"We need to assess the damage," Evelyn said, trying to keep her voice steady. "See if we can get the systems back online and figure out where we are."

Harris nodded, pushing himself to his feet with their help. "Agreed. We need to know what we're dealing with. Let's get the crew on their feet and see what we can salvage."

As they worked to rouse the remaining crew members, Evelyn couldn't shake the sense of unease that had settled over her. Something about the silence felt wrong, unnatural, as if they were in a place where sound itself was muted by an unseen force. The air was thick with an oppressive weight, and the shadows seemed to cling to the corners of the room, refusing to be dispelled by the emergency lights.

Once everyone was conscious and as stable as they could be given the circumstances, Captain Harris issued orders to start a full diagnostic of the ship's systems. The crew moved with a sense of urgency; their fear palpable but held in check by the need to survive.

"Can we get any readings from outside?" Evelyn asked one of the engineers, a young man named Collins who was working frantically to bring up the external sensors.

Collins shook his head, frustration etched on his face. "I'm trying, but the systems are barely functioning. Whatever hit us fried a lot of the electronics. I can't get anything beyond the basic life support systems."

"What about the engines?" Captain Harris asked, joining them. "Can we move?"

"I'm working on that, sir," Collins replied. "But it's not looking good. We're dead in the water until we can get the main power back online."

Evelyn felt a knot of fear tighten in her chest. They were stranded in the middle of the Bermuda Triangle, with no power, no way to move, and no way to communicate with the outside world. And they were completely at the mercy of whatever force had attacked them.

"We need to get the backup systems operational," Evelyn said, trying to push down the rising panic. "If we can at least get some power restored, we might be able to figure out where we are and what we're dealing with."

"I'll see what I can do," Collins said, already turning back to his work.

Harris looked at Evelyn, his expression grim. "We need answers, and we need them fast. We can't stay here, whatever that structure is, it's too dangerous. We need to find a way out of here before it's too late."

Evelyn nodded, though she had no idea how they were going to accomplish that. They were trapped, with no clear way forward, and the longer they stayed, the more vulnerable they became. But she couldn't let herself dwell on that, not now. They had to keep moving, keep fighting, or they were as good as dead.

Hours passed as the crew worked tirelessly to assess the damage and restore some semblance of order to the ship. The main power remained offline, but they managed to bring up a few critical systems on the backups, including life support and basic navigational sensors. But the news was grim—the Nautilus was heavily damaged, and without full power, they were essentially drifting in the water, vulnerable to whatever forces were at play.

Evelyn spent most of her time on the bridge, working alongside Sarah and Captain Harris to piece together what had happened. The structure's energy field had created some kind of temporal or spatial distortion of that much they were certain. But beyond that, the data was too fragmented to draw any definitive conclusions.

"We're not getting any external readings," Sarah said, her voice tinged with frustration as she studied the sensor data. "It's like

we're in a bubble no signals, no radio waves, nothing. It's just…
blank."

Captain Harris frowned. "Could the structure have trapped us
in some kind of anomaly?"

"It's possible," Evelyn said, though the thought filled her with
dread. "But if that's the case, we need to figure out how to get out
of it. We can't just sit here and wait for rescue."

"Agreed," Harris said. "But until we know more, our options
are limited. We need to focus on getting the engines back online
and finding a way to communicate with the outside world."

Evelyn nodded, though a nagging thought lingered at the back
of her mind. There was something they were missing some crucial
piece of the puzzle that could explain what had happened and how
to escape it. But the harder she tried to grasp it, the more elusive
it became, like a word on the tip of her tongue that refused to be
spoken.

As the hours dragged on, exhaustion began to take its toll on
the crew. Most of them had been working non-stop since the
incident, their nerves frayed by the constant tension and the
oppressive atmosphere that hung over the ship. Evelyn could see
it in their eyes the fear, the uncertainty, the growing sense of
hopelessness.

They were all thinking the same thing, though no one dared to say it aloud: What if they were already dead? What if this was some kind of purgatory, a place where the lost souls of the Bermuda Triangle were condemned to drift forever?

Evelyn shook off the thought, refusing to give in to despair. They were still alive, still fighting, as long as they had breath in their bodies, there was hope. But that hope was growing thinner with each passing hour, stretched to the breaking point by the relentless pressure of the unknown.

"Evelyn," Sarah's voice broke through her reverie, pulling her back to the present. "We're picking up something faint, but it's there."

Evelyn's heart skipped a beat as she turned to the console where Sarah was working. "What is it? A signal?"

"I'm not sure," Sarah said, frowning as she adjusted the controls. "It's weak barely registering on the sensors. But it's consistent, like a pulse. I'm trying to lock onto it."

Captain Harris moved closer, his expression tense. "Could it be a distress signal?"

"It's possible," Sarah said, though she didn't sound convinced. "But it's strange it doesn't match any known frequency. It's almost like... like it's coming from inside the ship."

Evelyn felt a chill run down her spine. "Inside? But how...?"

Before she could finish the thought, the lights flickered again, and the ship was rocked by another jolt, though less violent than the first. The pulse on the sensors grew stronger, more defined, as if responding to the ship's movement.

"What the hell is going on?" Captain Harris muttered, his eyes narrowing as he studied the data.

Evelyn's mind raced, trying to make sense of the anomaly. Could it be a malfunction? Or was there something or someone on board the Nautilus that they hadn't accounted for?

"Let's not jump to conclusions," Captain Harris said, though his voice was tight with unease. "It could be a glitch in the system, a feedback loop from the damaged electronics.
But we can't ignore it. We need to investigate."

Evelyn nodded, though the knot in her stomach tightened. "I'll check the lower decks, see if I can trace the source of the signal."

"I'll go with you," Sarah offered, though her voice wavered slightly. She was clearly just as uneasy as Evelyn, but she wasn't about to let her friend go down there alone.

Captain Harris nodded. "Take Collins with you. I'll stay here and monitor the readings. And keep your comms open,
I want to know the moment you find anything."

With a shared look of determination, Evelyn, Sarah, and Collins left the bridge and headed down to the lower decks, where the pulse was strongest. The ship was eerily silent as they made their way through the corridors, the emergency lights casting long, flickering shadows that danced on the walls.

As they descended deeper into the ship, the air grew colder, the oppressive atmosphere pressing down on them like a physical weight. The pulse grew louder in their ears, a low, rhythmic thrum that seemed to resonate through their bones.

"Do you hear that?" Collins asked, his voice barely above a whisper.

Evelyn nodded, her grip tightening on the flashlight in her hand. "It's getting stronger. We're close."

They reached the engineering deck, where the pulse was almost deafening. The room was filled with the hum of machinery, but the main power core was dark, its usual glow replaced by a cold, lifeless metal. The pulse seemed to be coming from behind a bulkhead at the far end of the room, where a thick metal door blocked their path.

"This is it," Evelyn said, her voice trembling slightly as she approached the door. "Whatever it is, it's behind here."

Collins swallowed hard, his face pale in the dim light. "Are you sure we want to open it?"

Evelyn hesitated, her hand hovering over the control panel. Every instinct in her body screamed at her to turn back, to leave whatever was behind that door alone. But she knew they couldn't. They needed answers, and this was their only lead.

"We have to," she said, though the words felt hollow in her mouth. "We need to know what's causing this."

With a deep breath, she pressed the button to unlock the door. The mechanism groaned in protest, but slowly, the door slid open, revealing the darkness beyond.

For a moment, they stood frozen, staring into the abyss. The pulse was deafening now, a relentless thrum that seemed to shake the very walls of the ship. And then, from the darkness, something moved.

Evelyn's heart leaped into her throat as she saw it, a figure, shrouded in shadow, stepping out from the gloom. It was tall, almost inhumanly so, its form indistinct in the dim light. But its eyes cold, piercing eyes that seemed to see right through her, glowed with an unnatural light.

"Who… who are you?" Evelyn whispered, her voice trembling with fear.

The figure didn't respond. Instead, it raised a hand, and the pulse stopped, plunging the room into an eerie silence. For a moment, the only sound was the ragged breathing of the three crewmembers, their eyes locked on the figure before them.

Then, in a voice that was both familiar and alien, the figure spoke. "You shouldn't have come here."

Evelyn's blood ran cold as the figure stepped closer, its eyes burning with an intensity that made her want to flee. But she couldn't move, couldn't speak, she was paralyzed by fear, held in place by the figure's gaze.

"We didn't... we didn't mean to," Sarah stammered, her voice barely above a whisper. "We were just... investigating."

The figure tilted its head, as if considering her words. "You have entered a place that is not meant for the living," it said, its voice echoing in the darkness. "This place... this triangle... it is a gateway, a boundary between worlds. Those who cross it are lost, forever adrift in the void."

Evelyn's mind raced, trying to comprehend the figure's words. A gateway? A boundary between worlds? It was impossible absurd. But everything they had experienced the energy surges, the temporal distortions, the eerie silence suggested that there was some truth to it.

"What... what do you want from us?" she managed to ask, her voice trembling.

The figure's eyes seemed to bore into her soul. "You seek to understand, but there are some things that are beyond comprehension. You are not the first to come here... and you will not be the last. But the longer you stay, the more you risk becoming like them."

"Like whom?" Collins asked, his voice shaking.

The figure didn't answer. Instead, it stepped back into the shadows, its form fading until it was nothing more than a silhouette. "Leave this place," it said, its voice growing faint. "Or be consumed by the darkness."

And then, with a final pulse of energy, the figure vanished, leaving them alone in the cold, empty room.

For a moment, none of them moved, too stunned to react. Then Evelyn finally found her voice. "We need to get back to the bridge," she said, her voice shaking. "We need to tell Captain Harris what we've seen."

Sarah and Collins nodded, too shocked to speak. Together, they hurried back through the corridors, the pulse gone but the oppressive weight still lingering in the air. As they reached the bridge, they found Captain Harris waiting for them, his expression grim.

"What did you find?" he asked, his eyes scanning their faces.

Evelyn took a deep breath, trying to steady her nerves. "We found… something. A figure it spoke to us. It said… it said this place is a gateway, a boundary between worlds."

Harris's eyes widened in disbelief. "A gateway? That's… that's impossible."

"I know it sounds crazy," Evelyn said, her voice urgent. "But it's the only explanation that makes sense. The energy surges, the temporal distortions… they're all symptoms of a crossing between dimensions. And if we stay here, we risk being trapped in this void forever."

Harris stared at her, his mind racing to process the information. "Then we have to find a way out before it's too late."

Evelyn nodded, though fear gnawed at her insides. The figure's words echoed in her mind, a chilling reminder of the stakes. They were caught in the grip of something beyond their understanding, and the only way to survive was to escape the triangle's deadly grasp.

But as she looked out at the dark waters surrounding the ship, she couldn't shake the feeling that they were already too late.

Chapter 8

Evelyn stood at the bridge, her thoughts swirling like the turbulent waters outside. The image of the figure from the lower deck was burned into her mind, those eyes, cold and all-knowing, and the cryptic warning it had delivered. The reality of their situation was sinking in, the weight of it pressing down on her chest like a vice. The Bermuda Triangle had always been a place of mystery and fear, but now, she knew it was more than that. It was a boundary, a gate between worlds, and they were dangerously close to crossing it.

Harris paced beside her, his jaw clenched, his mind clearly racing. The crew around them worked in tense silence, their fear palpable in the air. Every so often, someone would glance at the dark screens or out the windows into the black void beyond, their expressions a mix of anxiety and dread.

"We have to find a way out," Harris said, breaking the silence. His voice was firm, but there was a trace of desperation that hadn't been there before. "We can't stay here much longer. That figure… whatever it was, it's right. We're not meant to be here."

Evelyn nodded, though she didn't know where to begin. The ship was barely functioning, the main engines offline, and the only power they had was from the failing backup systems. The eerie silence outside was broken only by the occasional groan of the ship's hull, a reminder of the relentless forces pressing in on them from all sides.

Sarah was at the main console, running diagnostics and trying to bring up any readings that might give them a clue as to where they were or how to escape. She looked up at Evelyn, her face pale and drawn. "I'm picking up something," she said, her voice tight. "It's faint, but it's there a weak signal, like an echo. It might be a way out."

Harris placed himself beside her, his expression intense. "Can you trace it? Where is it coming from?"

"I'm trying," Sarah replied, her fingers flying over the controls. "But the signal is unstable it's like it's being distorted by whatever's around us. It could be a ship, or… or something else."

Evelyn leaned over her shoulder, studying the data on the screen. The signal was erratic, flickering in and out like a dying heartbeat. But it was their only lead, their only hope of escaping this nightmare.

"We have to follow it," Evelyn said, determination hardening her voice. "It might lead us out of this void."

Harris nodded. "Agreed. Sarah, do whatever you can to lock onto that signal. We'll follow it, but we need to be ready for anything. This could be a trap, or it could be our only chance. Either way, we can't stay here."

The decision made, the crew sprang into action, working to get the ship moving despite the odds. The engines groaned as they were coaxed back to life, sputtering and stalling before finally catching, the Nautilus lurching forward into the darkness.

The journey through the void was unlike anything they had ever experienced. The water outside was pitch black, the usual currents and waves replaced by an eerie stillness. It felt as though they were moving through a vast, empty space, where the normal rules of physics no longer applied. The ship's sensors were useless, unable to penetrate the thick shroud that surrounded them.

Evelyn couldn't shake the feeling that they were being watched that the figure from the lower decks or something even more sinister was lurking just beyond their reach, waiting for the right moment to strike. Every creak of the hull, every flicker of the lights, set her nerves on edge, the tension in the air so thick it was suffocating.

As they moved deeper into the darkness, the signal grew stronger, more defined. It wasn't a straight path rather, it seemed to twist and turn, leading them through a labyrinth of unseen forces. The ship lurched and groaned with every shift, as if fighting against an invisible current.

"Steady as she goes," Harris ordered, his voice calm but commanding. "We don't know what's ahead, but we're not turning back."

Evelyn kept her eyes on the screen, watching as the signal slowly resolved into something more concrete. It was still weak, but there was a pattern to it now, a rhythm that seemed to pulse in time with the ship's movements.

"I think it's a beacon," Sarah said, her voice filled with a mix of hope and uncertainty. "Some kind of navigational marker, but it's old, really old. It might be from another ship that got caught here, or… or something else entirely."

"A beacon?" Harris echoed, his brow furrowing. "That could mean someone, or something has been here before us. Maybe they found a way out."

"Or maybe they didn't," Evelyn murmured, the words slipping out before she could stop them. The idea that others had been trapped here, lost in the void, sent a shiver down her spine. What had happened to them? Were they doomed to suffer the same fate?

The Nautilus pressed on; the signal growing stronger with each passing minute. But with that strength came a new threat a distortion in the water ahead, a rippling in the void that set the ship swaying dangerously. The lights flickered, and the hull groaned louder, the pressure building as they moved closer to the source of the signal.

"We're hitting some kind of turbulence," Collins reported from his station, his voice strained. "It's not like anything I've ever seen like the water itself is fighting against us."

"Hold course," Harris ordered, though his knuckles were white as he gripped the console. "We can't afford to lose that signal now. If we back off, we might not find it again."

Evelyn's heart pounded in her chest as the ship bucked and heaved, the distortion growing stronger, more violent. It felt as though they were being pulled into a whirlpool, the ship groaning under the strain.

"We can't hold this course much longer!" Collins shouted, his voice rising in panic. "The hull can't take it!"

"Just a little further," Sarah urged, her eyes locked on the screen. "We're so close, I can feel it."

But the distortion was too strong. With a final, deafening groan, the Nautilus was wrenched off course, spinning wildly as it was caught in the pull of the anomaly. The crew was thrown from their stations, the ship lurching violently as it was dragged deeper into the void.

Evelyn clung to the console, her heart racing as the ship was buffeted by unseen forces. The signal on the screen flickered, growing fainter, then stronger, as if caught in the same vortex that was tearing the Nautilus apart.

"We're going to be torn to pieces!" someone screamed, their voice barely audible over the roar of the ship's straining hull.

Harris tried to regain control, shouting orders as the crew scrambled to stabilize the ship. But it was no use the Nautilus was caught in the grip of something far beyond their understanding, something that defied all logic and reason.

Evelyn felt the pull of the anomaly tugging at her very soul, the pressure in the room growing so intense it was hard to breathe. The ship's systems flickered, the lights dimming as the power drained away, leaving them in near-total darkness.

"We're losing power!" Collins yelled; his voice filled with panic. "We're going down!"

Evelyn's thoughts raced, her mind grasping for any solution, any way out. But there was no escape, no way to fight against the overwhelming force that was dragging them down.

Just when it seemed the ship would be crushed under the pressure, a blinding light filled the bridge, so bright it burned into Evelyn's retinas. She cried out, throwing her hands up to shield her eyes, but the light was everywhere, surrounding them, consuming them.

And then, just as suddenly as it had come, the light vanished, leaving them in darkness once more.

Evelyn blinked, her vision slowly adjusting to the dim emergency lights that flickered back on. The ship was still, the violent shaking gone, replaced by an eerie silence that seemed to press in from all sides.

"What… what happened?" Sarah whispered, her voice trembling with fear and confusion.

Evelyn looked around, her heart pounding. The crew was still at their stations, all of them as disoriented as she felt. But the ship was intact, and the distortion that had been tearing them apart was gone.

"I don't know," Evelyn said, her voice hoarse. "But… I think we're still alive."

Harris was the first to regain his composure, barking orders as the crew scrambled to assess the situation. "Status report! Where are we? What's our condition?"

Collins was already at his station, frantically working the controls. "Engines are offline, but the hull is intact. No major breaches. But we're… we're not where we were before."

Evelyn's stomach dropped at his words. "What do you mean?"

Collins turned to face them, his expression one of utter disbelief. "We've been… we've been moved. I don't know how, but we're in a completely different location miles from where we were before. And the signal it's stronger now, but it's coming from… from inside the ship."

The air on the bridge grew heavy with tension as his words sank in. The signal, the beacon they had been following was no longer outside in the void. It was here, with them, inside the Nautilus.

Evelyn's mind reeled; the implications too terrifying to fully comprehend. Had they brought something back with them? Or had the ship itself become part of the anomaly, forever tied to the dark forces that ruled this cursed place?

Harris stared at the data, his face pale. "We need to find out what's causing that signal, and we need to do it now. Whatever it is, it's the key to understanding what's happening to us."

Evelyn nodded, though fear gnawed at her insides. The encounter with the figure in the lower decks had been harrowing enough, but this was something else entirely. They were no longer just investigating the mystery of the Bermuda Triangle. They were part of it now, woven into its dark, twisted fabric.

As the crew prepared to search the ship, Evelyn couldn't shake the feeling that whatever they found next would change everything. The pulse of the signal thrummed in the air, a haunting reminder that they were not alone and that the true horror of the Triangle had only just begun.

Chapter 9

The oppressive weight of the unknown hung heavily in the air as Evelyn and the crew moved cautiously through the corridors of the Nautilus. The ship's dim emergency lights flickered intermittently, casting eerie shadows that seemed to pulse in time with the mysterious signal now emanating from within the vessel. Each step was accompanied by the creaking of the ship's metal framework, the sounds echoing through the silent halls, reminding them of the fragile barrier between their world and the abyss outside.

Evelyn's thoughts were a chaotic swirl as she led the way, her mind replaying the events that had brought them to this point. The strange figure they had encountered, the blinding light, and the sudden, disorienting shift in their location all of it defied logic, leaving her grasping at straws to make sense of it. But deep down, she knew there was no rational explanation for what they were experiencing. They were far beyond the boundaries of the known world, in a place where reason held no sway.

Sarah and Collins followed closely behind, their faces pale with fear and uncertainty. The tension between them was palpable, each of them aware that whatever lay ahead could be the key to their survival or their doom. Captain Harris, despite his stoic demeanor, had lost some of his usual composure. He kept one hand on his holstered weapon, the other clenched into a tight fist as if ready to fight whatever malevolent force had invaded his ship.

As they approached the source of the signal, Evelyn's pulse quickened. The corridor they were in led to the ship's central cargo hold a cavernous space that had been mostly untouched since they had set out on this ill-fated journey. The closer they got, the more intense the signal became, a low, thrumming hum that vibrated through the walls and floor, as if the ship itself was resonating with the sound.

Evelyn exchanged a nervous glance with Sarah as they reached the heavy steel door that led into the hold. The pulse was almost deafening now, and the very air seemed to vibrate with a strange energy that made the hairs on the back of Evelyn's neck stand on end. She could feel it deep in her bones, a primal warning that whatever was on the other side of this door was something she should fear.

Harris moved forward, his expression grim. "Stay alert," he ordered, his voice low and tense. "We don't know what we're dealing with, but we need answers. And we need to be ready for anything."

Evelyn nodded, steeling herself for what was to come. She could see the same resolve in Sarah's eyes, despite the fear that lingered there. Collins was visibly shaking, but he held his ground, clutching his equipment tightly as if it could somehow protect him from whatever awaited them.

With a deep breath, Harris keyed in the access code, and the heavy door slid open with a slow, grinding noise. The pulse immediately intensified, the sound so loud now that it seemed to reverberate through their skulls. Evelyn winced, pressing a hand to her ear as they stepped into the cargo hold.

The hold was bathed in a strange, otherworldly light that seemed to emanate from nowhere and everywhere at once. The walls and floor were covered in a shimmering, translucent substance that pulsed in rhythm with the signal, as if the very fabric of the ship had been transformed by the presence of whatever was inside. The air was thick with a strange, almost metallic scent that made Evelyn's stomach churn.

In the centre of the hold, surrounded by the strange substance, was a large, pulsating mass. It was amorphous, constantly shifting and changing shape, as if it were alive and breathing. The light seemed to originate from within it, pulsing in time with the signal that had drawn them here. Evelyn's breath caught in her throat as she stared at it, a sense of overwhelming dread settling over her like a suffocating blanket.

"What... what is that?" Collins whispered, his voice barely audible over the thrum of the pulse.

"No idea," Harris replied, though his voice was tight with tension. "But it's not something I've ever seen before."

Evelyn took a cautious step forward, her eyes fixed on the pulsating mass. She could feel the energy coming off it, a tangible force that seemed to press against her skin, making her feel simultaneously drawn to it and repelled by it. The closer she got, the stronger the sensation became, until it was almost unbearable.

Suddenly, the mass convulsed, its form shifting and contorting as if in response to her presence. Evelyn froze, her heart pounding in her chest as she watched it twist and writhe. The light intensified, flaring brightly before dimming again, and for a moment, she thought she could see something within the mass something dark and indistinct, like a shadow moving just out of sight.

"We should fall back," Sarah said, her voice trembling. "We don't know what that thing is, it could be dangerous." But Evelyn couldn't move. She was transfixed, her gaze locked on the shifting mass. There was something about it, something familiar yet completely alien, that she couldn't tear herself away from. It was as if the mass was calling to her, beckoning her closer, drawing her in with an invisible force she couldn't resist.

"Evelyn, we need to go," Harris urged, his tone more forceful. "Now."

But before she could respond, the mass suddenly split open, revealing a dark void at its center. Evelyn gasped as the light within it flared, blindingly bright, and a surge of energy burst from the void, sweeping over her like a tidal wave. She cried out, stumbling back as the force of it knocked her off her feet.

The light consumed her vision, and for a moment, she felt herself being pulled into the void, as if the very essence of her being was being torn from her body. She could hear the others shouting, could feel hands grabbing at her, trying to pull her back, but it was as if she were trapped in a different dimension, unable to escape the pull of the mass.

And then, just as suddenly as it had started, it was over. The light vanished, and Evelyn found herself lying on the cold, metal floor of the cargo hold, gasping for breath. The pulsating mass was gone, replaced by an eerie stillness that hung heavy in the air. The others were around her, their faces pale and stricken with fear, but they were all unharmed.

"What... what happened?" Evelyn managed to choke out, her voice weak and shaky.

Sarah knelt beside her, her eyes wide with concern. "You were... you were pulled toward it, like it was trying to take you. We tried to pull you back, but you were... you were almost gone."

Harris's expression was grim as he helped her to her feet. "Whatever that thing was, it's gone now. But it left something behind."

Evelyn followed his gaze to the spot where the pulsating mass had been. In its place was a small, dark object, barely larger than a fist. It was smooth and perfectly round, with a faint, iridescent sheen that seemed to shift and change as she looked at it. The object pulsed faintly, in time with the signal that had drawn them here, as if it were a living thing.

"What is that?" Collins asked, his voice trembling.

"I don't know," Evelyn replied, though she couldn't shake the feeling that the object was somehow important crucial, even, to understanding what had happened to them. "But we need to take it back to the lab. Whatever it is, it might be the key to getting us out of here."

Harris nodded, though there was a shadow of doubt in his eyes.

"Be careful with it. We don't know what we're dealing with, and I don't want any more surprises."

Evelyn gingerly picked up the object, cradling it in her hands. It was surprisingly warm to the touch, and as she held it, she could feel a faint vibration, like a heartbeat, pulsing through it. The sensation was unsettling, but she forced herself to focus. They were running out of time, and this might be their only chance to escape the Bermuda Triangle's grasp.

As they made their way back to the lab, the ship was eerily silent, the oppressive atmosphere still lingering in the air. The object pulsed steadily in Evelyn's hands, its rhythm matching the faint signal that still emanated from it. She couldn't shake the feeling that they were being watched that the presence that had manifested in the cargo hold was still with them, lurking just out of sight.

When they reached the lab, Evelyn carefully placed the object on the examination table. The others gathered around, their faces tense with anticipation as she began to analyse it. The equipment hummed to life, the screens flickering with data as she scanned the object, searching for any clue as to what it was or where it had come from.

But the more she analysed it, the less sense it made. The object defied all conventional logic it wasn't made of any known material, and its energy signature was unlike anything she had ever encountered. It was as if it had come from another world, a place beyond the boundaries of their reality.

"This doesn't make any sense," Evelyn muttered, frustration gnawing at her. "It's like it's alive, but not in any way we understand. It's almost like it's... waiting."

"Waiting for what?" Sarah asked, her voice filled with apprehension.

"I don't know," Evelyn replied, shaking her head. "But whatever it is, it's connected to the Bermuda Triangle and to us. It's like it's a part of this place, or maybe it's the key to controlling it."

Harris leaned in closer, his eyes narrowing as he studied the object. "Then we need to figure out how to use it fast. If this thing can help us get out of here, we can't afford to waste any more time."

Evelyn nodded, though a sense of unease gnawed at her. The object pulsed steadily, its rhythm like a countdown, a reminder that they were running out of time. But there was something else, too—a sense of inevitability, as if the object was leading them toward a final confrontation with the forces that controlled this place.

As she worked, Evelyn couldn't shake the feeling that the object was somehow alive, aware of their presence, and that it was guiding them toward something that would change everything they thought they knew about the Bermuda Triangle, and about reality itself.

And as the minutes ticked by, the ship's hull creaking and groaning in the oppressive silence, Evelyn realized with a sinking heart that they were no longer just investigating the mysteries of the Bermuda Triangle. They were now part of those mysteries, inextricably linked to the dark forces that ruled this place.

And there was no turning back.

Chapter 10

The lab was a claustrophobic haven of blinking monitors and humming machinery, its walls lined with the paraphernalia of scientific inquiry. Evelyn's hands moved with practiced precision as she continued to analyse the mysterious object on the table. The dim glow of the lab's emergency lights cast long, distorted shadows that danced across the walls, adding to the oppressive atmosphere.

Harris and the rest of the crew stood around the table, their faces a mixture of anxiety and curiosity. Sarah, her eyes wide with a mixture of fear and fascination, watched as Evelyn ran the latest series of scans. Collins was pacing back and forth, his anxiety palpable, while Captain Harris tried to maintain an air of calm control, though his clenched fists and furrowed brow betrayed his inner turmoil.

"What are we looking at?" Sarah asked, her voice barely above a whisper. "What does it mean?"

Evelyn paused, glancing up from the readout. The data was bewildering patterns and signatures that defied any known scientific explanation. The object's surface seemed to shift subtly, its iridescent sheen changing in a mesmerizing, almost hypnotic manner. Despite her training, Evelyn felt a creeping sense of dread, as if the object was somehow alive, feeding off their fear.

"It's unlike anything I've ever seen," Evelyn said, her voice tense. "The object's material is completely unknown, and its energy signature… it's like it's reacting to us. It's almost as if it's… aware."

"Awareness?" Collins echoed, his face pale. "Are you saying this thing is alive?"

"I don't know," Evelyn admitted, shaking her head. "But it seems to have some kind of sentience. The way it responds to our presence, to our fear, it's as if it's feeding off our emotions."

Harris moved closer to the table; his gaze fixed on the object. "If it's alive, then it's possible it's connected to whatever force is controlling the Bermuda Triangle. It might be the key to understanding what's happening to us."

The thought sent a chill down Evelyn's spine. The idea of a sentient object controlling or influencing their reality was terrifying, but it was the only explanation that seemed to fit the strange occurrences they had encountered.

"Whatever it is," Harris continued, "we need to find out how to control it. If it's linked to the Bermuda Triangle, it might be able to help us navigate or even escape."

Evelyn nodded, though her mind was racing. The pulsating rhythm of the object seemed to synchronize with her own heartbeat, each pulse sending a shiver down her spine. She had the distinct feeling that time was running out, and that they were on the brink of discovering something both profoundly significant and profoundly dangerous.

"I'll run a series of tests," Evelyn said, her voice firm. "Maybe we can determine if the object can communicate with us, or if it responds to specific stimuli."

As Evelyn worked, her hands moved almost mechanically, her mind consumed by the task at hand. The scans revealed strange fluctuations in the object's energy field, patterns that seemed to shift and change with each passing moment. The object's surface appeared to ripple, as if it were reacting to her every touch.

Hours passed in a blur of activity. The lab was filled with the soft hum of machinery and the occasional crackle of static from the communication equipment. The crew's exhaustion was palpable, but they remained focused, driven by the desperate hope that the object held the key to their escape.

Evelyn's concentration was broken by a sudden, sharp hiss from one of the monitors. She looked up to see the object's energy signature spike dramatically, a brilliant flash of light momentarily illuminating the lab. The light was blinding, and for a moment, Evelyn felt as if she were falling into a vast, empty void.

"Look!" Sarah cried out, her voice filled with awe and fear. "It's changing!"

Evelyn squinted through the afterimages of the flash, trying to make sense of what she was seeing. The object had transformed, its shape becoming more defined, almost crystalline. It pulsed with a rhythmic, almost hypnotic pattern, and the light that emanated from it seemed to form intricate patterns in the air.

"Is it... trying to communicate?" Collins asked, his voice trembling with a mix of curiosity and trepidation.

"I think so," Evelyn replied, her eyes locked on the object. "It's as if it's trying to show us something."

The patterns in the air coalesced into a series of symbols and images, shifting and morphing with an almost liquid grace. The symbols were alien, intricate and beautiful, and they seemed to convey a message—a warning, perhaps, or a guide. Evelyn could feel a strange resonance in the air, as if the symbols were resonating with something deep within her.

"What is it saying?" Harris asked, his voice taut with tension.

Evelyn studied the symbols, her brow furrowing in concentration. The images seemed to depict a series of events, a journey through darkness and light, a struggle between forces beyond comprehension. There were images of ships, of storms and calm seas, and of a vast, dark chasm that seemed to represent the Bermuda Triangle itself.

"It's… it's showing us a path," Evelyn said, her voice filled with wonder. "A way through the darkness, a way to navigate the Triangle. But it's also showing us something else—something about the forces that control this place."

As she spoke, the symbols shifted again, forming a new image—a pair of eyes, dark and unblinking, watching from the void. The eyes seemed to convey a sense of malevolence, a warning of a presence that was both ancient and powerful.

"This…" Evelyn said, her voice trembling, "this is a warning. It's telling us that there is something watching us, something that controls the Triangle. And if we don't follow its guidance, we might be lost forever."

Harris's expression hardened. "Then we need to follow the path it's showing us. If it's our only chance to escape, we must take it."

Evelyn nodded, though a sense of unease gnawed at her insides. The object was their only hope, but it was also a symbol of the unknown, of the dark forces that governed the Bermuda Triangle. As they prepared to follow the path laid out by the object, Evelyn couldn't shake the feeling that they were walking into a trap, that the forces controlling the Triangle had been waiting for them all along.

With a deep breath, Evelyn gathered the crew and prepared to follow the instructions provided by the object. They moved through the ship, guided by the shifting patterns of light and symbols, each step filled with a mixture of hope and dread.

The ship's corridors seemed to stretch and twist, the very walls bending and warping as they followed the path laid out by the object. The air grew colder, and the shadows seemed to lengthen, as if the ship itself was becoming part of the dark, enigmatic force that surrounded them.

As they reached the destination, a sense of anticipation hung heavy in the air. Evelyn could feel the pulsating energy of the object guiding them, leading them toward a final confrontation with the forces that controlled the Bermuda Triangle. The symbols had led them here, but what awaited them was still a mystery.

In the dim light of the corridor, Evelyn took a deep breath, her heart pounding in her chest. The object's rhythmic pulse seemed to synchronize with her own heartbeat, each thrum a reminder of the stakes involved.

"Ready?" Harris asked, his voice steady but filled with tension.

Evelyn nodded, though her mind was a whirlwind of fear and determination. "Let's do this."

With a final, resolute glance at the object, Evelyn and the crew stepped forward, ready to face whatever lay ahead. The Bermuda

Triangle had revealed its path, and now they had to follow it, no matter where it might lead.

Chapter 11

The atmosphere on the Nautilus had shifted from tense anticipation to a palpable sense of dread. The ship seemed to pulse with an unsettling energy as Evelyn and the crew moved through the dimly lit corridors, their path illuminated only by the eerie glow of the mysterious object. Each step felt like a step deeper into an unknown abyss, the sense of being watched growing stronger with every passing moment.

Evelyn's heart pounded in her chest, each beat echoing in her ears. The object, now nestled in a secure container that she carried with trembling hands, seemed to hum with a life of its own. The pulsing light it emitted cast long shadows on the walls, creating an atmosphere that was both mesmerizing and terrifying. Evelyn's mind raced, her thoughts a jumbled mess of fear and determination. The symbols, the warning of the dark presence, and the strange, rhythmic energy all combined to create a sense of imminent danger.

She glanced at Harris, whose face was etched with a grim resolve. The captain's usually stern demeanor was tempered with a flicker of anxiety. He led the way, his footsteps echoing loudly in the quiet corridor. Sarah followed closely behind, her face pale and eyes wide, while Collins trailed, his anxiety barely contained. The tension among them was palpable, each person grappling with their own fears as they ventured into the unknown.

As they moved forward, the corridors seemed to stretch and twist, the ship itself appearing to shift around them. The walls were lined with an eerie, pulsating light that seemed to distort their perception of space. It was as if the very fabric of reality was unraveling, leaving them disoriented and uncertain of their surroundings. Evelyn's stomach churned with a mix of fear and nausea. Every shadow seemed to hold a hidden threat, and every sound was magnified into an ominous portent.

"Are we sure this is the right way?" Sarah's voice broke the silence, her tone trembling with apprehension. "This place… it's changing."

"We have to follow the path," Captain Harris replied, his voice steady but with an edge of weariness. "The object led us here. We have to trust it."

Evelyn's thoughts mirrored Sarah's unease. The object had provided them with a path, but what lay at the end of it was still a mystery. The sense of being watched, of something lurking just beyond their vision, was overwhelming. It was as if the Bermuda Triangle itself was alive, its dark presence suffusing every corner of the ship.

They reached a heavy metal door, its surface etched with strange symbols that seemed to pulse in time with the object's rhythmic light. Captain Harris took a deep breath and keyed in the access code. The door slid open with a groan, revealing a chamber bathed in a dim, shifting light that seemed to emanate from the very walls.

The room was vast, with a high ceiling that was lost in shadow. In the center of the chamber stood a strange, crystalline structure, its surface shimmering with the same iridescent light that had emanated from the object. The structure seemed to pulse with a rhythmic energy, resonating with the same frequency as the object Evelyn held.

Evelyn walked into the room; her senses overwhelmed by the strange, otherworldly ambiance. The air was thick with an almost tangible energy, a crackling sensation that made her skin prickle. She could feel the vibrations in her bones, a deep, unsettling resonance that seemed to seep into her very being.

The crystalline structure was mesmerizing, its surface shifting and changing as if it were alive. The light that emanated from it was both beautiful and haunting, casting eerie patterns on the walls and floor. Evelyn felt a shiver run down her spine as she approached it, the rhythmic pulsing of the structure matching the beat of her own heart.

"This is it," Harris said, his voice reverent. "The object led us here. This must be the source of the signal."

Evelyn nodded, though her mind was a whirl of conflicting emotions. She was both awed and terrified by the crystalline structure. It was clear that it was a focal point of the Bermuda Triangle's dark energy, but its purpose remained unclear.

She carefully placed the object on a nearby pedestal, its rhythmic pulsing blending with the energy of the crystalline structure. The room seemed to hum with a newfound intensity, the light growing brighter and more erratic. Evelyn could feel a pressure building in the air, a sense of anticipation and dread that was almost overwhelming.

As the object settled into place, the crystalline structure began to resonate more intensely. The light grew brighter, and the energy in the room became almost unbearable. Evelyn could feel her heart racing, her breath coming in short, shallow gasps. The walls of the chamber seemed to close in, the air growing heavy and charged with a palpable sense of foreboding.

"Is it doing something?" Collins asked, his voice trembling.

"I don't know," Evelyn replied, her gaze fixed on the crystalline structure. "But whatever it is, it's responding to the object."

The structure began to shift and change, its surface morphing into intricate patterns and symbols. The light pulsated in a rapid, erratic rhythm, and the energy in the room grew more intense. Evelyn felt a surge of panic as the chamber seemed to warp and distort around them, the boundaries of reality becoming increasingly fluid.

Suddenly, a blinding flash of light erupted from the crystalline structure, filling the room with a searing brilliance. Evelyn cried out, shielding her eyes as the intensity of the light overwhelmed her senses. The heat was almost unbearable, and she could feel a force pulling at her, as if trying to tear her away from the chamber.

Through the haze of light, she could see shapes moving, dark and indistinct. The sense of being watched intensified, and she could feel the presence of something ancient and powerful, a force that had been waiting for them. The walls of the chamber seemed to ripple and shift, and the very fabric of reality seemed to be unraveling.

The light slowly began to fade, leaving the room in an eerie, twilight glow. Evelyn lowered her hands, her eyes adjusting to the dim light. The crystalline structure had changed, its surface now covered with intricate, glowing symbols. The object on the pedestal was vibrating with a rhythmic pulse, its light synchronizing with the symbols on the structure.

"What just happened?" Sarah asked, her voice trembling.

"I'm not sure," Evelyn replied, her voice shaky. "But it looks like the structure is… responding to the object."

Harris stepped forward; his gaze fixed on the glowing symbols. "What do they mean?"

Evelyn studied the symbols, her mind racing to make sense of them. They seemed to form a complex pattern, a series of interlocking shapes and lines that conveyed a sense of movement and transition. It was as if the symbols were telling a story, a narrative of struggle and transformation.

"I think," Evelyn said slowly, "The symbols are a map maybe a guide. They seem to show a path through the Triangle, a way to navigate its dangers. But they also seem to convey a warning."

"A warning?" Harris repeated, his voice filled with concern.

"Yes," Evelyn replied, her voice tight. "It's like the Triangle itself is alive, and it's warning us about something.... something that's watching us, waiting for us."

The sense of foreboding was palpable, and Evelyn could feel the weight of the warning pressing down on her. The symbols seemed to shimmer with a dark energy, their glow casting long, shifting shadows that danced across the walls. It was as if the chamber itself was alive, reacting to their presence, and Evelyn couldn't shake the feeling that they were on the brink of something profoundly significant and profoundly dangerous.

"Whatever it is," Harris said, his voice resolute, "We need to figure out what these symbols mean. If they can help us navigate the Triangle, they might be our only chance to escape."

Evelyn nodded, though her mind was clouded with a sense of dread. The symbols were a guide, but they were also a warning, a reminder that they were dealing with forces beyond their understanding. The Bermuda Triangle was a place of darkness and mystery, and whatever lay ahead was still shrouded in uncertainty.

As the crew gathered around the pedestal, studying the glowing symbols, Evelyn felt a surge of determination. They had come this far, and they were not about to turn back now. The path ahead was fraught with danger, but they had to follow it, no matter where it might lead.

With a deep breath, Evelyn focused on the symbols, her mind racing to decipher their meaning. The Bermuda Triangle had revealed its secrets, but the true challenge lay in understanding and navigating them. The journey ahead would be perilous, but it was their only hope of escape and their only chance to uncover the truth about the dark forces that controlled the Triangle.

Chapter 12

The chamber was quiet except for the rhythmic hum of the crystalline structure and the soft, uneasy murmurs of the crew. Evelyn stood before the pedestal; her gaze fixed on the glowing symbols that had appeared on the crystalline structure. The intricate patterns shifted and morphed, revealing new details with each passing moment. The air was thick with tension, and Evelyn could feel her pulse quicken as she tried to make sense of the symbols.

Captain Harris, Sarah, and Collins clustered around the pedestal; their faces illuminated by the eerie glow of the symbols. The symbols were an enigmatic mix of shapes and lines, their meanings elusive but undeniably significant. The soft glow cast by the symbols created a mesmerizing, almost hypnotic effect, heightening the sense of mystery and foreboding.

Evelyn's mind raced as she studied the patterns, her thoughts tangled in a web of fear and determination. The symbols seemed to tell a story, a narrative that was both ancient and cryptic. She could sense that they were more than mere decorations they were a guide, a map that held the key to navigating the Bermuda Triangle.

The symbols began to shift, forming a new pattern that seemed to highlight a particular sequence of shapes. Evelyn's breath caught in her throat as she realized that the sequence appeared to form a route a path through the darkness of the Triangle. Her heart pounded in her chest as she tried to decipher the meaning behind the symbols.

"Captain," Evelyn said, her voice trembling with a mixture of excitement and apprehension, "I think we have a route. The symbols seem to show a path through the Triangle a way to navigate its dangers."

Harris stepped closer, his eyes narrowing as he examined the symbols. "Are you sure?"

"Yes," Evelyn replied, nodding vigorously. "The symbols... they seem to be guiding us. But there's something else.... something about a force that's watching us."

The room fell silent as the gravity of Evelyn's words sank in. The idea of a dark, malevolent force lurking within the Triangle was a chilling one, and it added a new layer of danger to their already perilous situation.

"Alright," Harris said, his voice steady despite the tension. "If this is a route, then we need to follow it. But we need to be cautious. We don't know what we might encounter."

Evelyn nodded, her hands trembling as she took a final look at the symbols. They seemed to be forming a series of coordinates or directions, a road map through the treacherous waters of the Triangle. The route appeared to lead through a series of dangerous and unpredictable zones, each one marked by symbols that conveyed a sense of peril and darkness.

As they prepared to follow the route, the chamber's atmosphere grew colder, and a sense of foreboding settled over them. The shadows seemed to stretch and deepen, and the air was filled with a palpable sense of anticipation. Evelyn could feel the weight of the unknown pressing down on her, and she took a deep breath to steady herself.

"Let's get moving," Harris said, his voice resolute. "We need to follow the route and see where it leads."

The crew moved with a sense of purpose, their steps echoing in the vast, shadowy chamber. Evelyn led the way, her gaze fixed on the symbols as they shifted and changed, guiding them toward the exit. The ship's corridors seemed to warp and twist around them, the very fabric of reality feeling as though it was in flux.

As they navigated through the ship, the sense of being watched grew stronger. The shadows seemed to move and shift, and the air was thick with a lingering sense of malevolence. Evelyn could feel the weight of unseen eyes on them, a constant reminder of the dark force that controlled the Bermuda Triangle.

"Do you hear that?" Sarah asked, her voice barely above a whisper.

Evelyn paused, listening intently. There was a faint, rhythmic sound, like a distant heartbeat or the thrum of machinery. It was faint but persistent, adding to the oppressive atmosphere that surrounded them.

"I hear it," Evelyn said, her voice tense. "It's getting louder."

The sound grew more distinct as they moved forward, the rhythmic pulse becoming more pronounced. It seemed to be coming from ahead, a steady, hypnotic beat that seemed to resonate with the symbols on the crystalline structure.

As they reached a large, open space, the source of the sound became apparent. The room was filled with a series of strange, mechanical devices, their surfaces covered in intricate patterns and symbols. The devices were arranged in a circular formation, and their rhythmic pulsing seemed to synchronize with the symbols on the crystalline structure.

Evelyn's eyes widened as she took in the sight. The devices appeared to be part of a larger mechanism; a complex array of machinery that seemed to be connected to the Bermuda Triangle's mysterious forces. The rhythmic sound was coming from the devices, their synchronized pulses creating a sense of eerie harmony.

"What is this place?" Collins asked, his voice filled with awe and apprehension.

"I'm not sure," Evelyn replied, her eyes scanning the machinery. "But it looks like some kind of control center maybe the heart of the Triangle's power."

As they approached the devices, the air grew colder, and a sense of dread settled over them. The symbols on the devices seemed to be glowing, their light reflecting off the surfaces of the machinery. Evelyn could feel the weight of the dark presence that had been watching them, its malevolent influence growing stronger.

The rhythmic pulsing of the devices grew louder, filling the room with a hypnotic resonance. Evelyn felt a strange sensation in her chest, as if the pulsing was somehow connected to her own heartbeat. She could feel her thoughts becoming muddled, her mind struggling to focus on the task at hand.

"Stay alert," Harris said, his voice steady despite the tension. "We don't know what we're dealing with."

Evelyn nodded, though her mind was clouded with a sense of unease. The machinery seemed to be part of a larger, more complex system, and she could feel the presence of the dark force that controlled the Triangle growing stronger.

As they moved closer to the central device, the symbols on its surface began to shift and change. The rhythmic pulsing grew more intense, and Evelyn could feel the energy in the room becoming almost unbearable. The light from the device cast long, shifting shadows, creating a sense of disorientation and unease.

Evelyn reached out to touch the device, her fingers trembling as she made contact. The surface was cold and smooth, and she could feel a faint vibration running through it. The symbols on the device seemed to respond to her touch, shifting and changing in a complex, mesmerizing pattern.

The device began to emit a soft, resonant hum, its rhythmic pulse becoming more pronounced. The air was filled with a strange energy, and Evelyn could feel her heart racing as the intensity of the pulse grew. The symbols on the device seemed to form a new pattern, a series of interconnected shapes and lines that conveyed a sense of movement and transition.

"This is incredible," Evelyn said, her voice filled with wonder and fear. "It's like the device is reacting to us, guiding us through the Triangle."

Harris stepped closer; his eyes fixed on the central device. "What's it showing us?"

Evelyn studied the new pattern, her mind racing to decipher its meaning. The symbols seemed to depict a series of events, a journey through the darkness of the Triangle. There were images of ships navigating treacherous waters, of storms and calm seas, and of a destination that was both mysterious and ominous.

"It's showing us a way out," Evelyn said, her voice trembling with a mix of hope and dread. "But it's also showing us the dangers we'll face along the way."

The symbols shifted again, forming a final image a dark, swirling vortex that seemed to represent the heart of the Bermuda Triangle. The vortex was surrounded by a web of symbols, each one conveying a sense of danger and uncertainty.

"This must be the centre of the Triangle," Evelyn said, her voice tight with tension. "The heart of its power. If we can reach it, we might be able to escape."

Harris nodded, his expression resolute. "Then we need to follow the route. We have to be prepared for whatever lies ahead."

The crew gathered their resolve, steeling themselves for the journey ahead. Evelyn took a deep breath, her mind filled with a mixture of fear and determination. The Bermuda Triangle had revealed its secrets, but the path to freedom was fraught with danger. They had to navigate through the darkness and face the forces that controlled the Triangle.

As they prepared to move forward, Evelyn glanced at the symbols one last time. The sense of foreboding was overwhelming, but she knew that they had no choice but to follow the path laid out before them. The journey ahead would be perilous, but it was their only chance to uncover the truth and escape the Bermuda Triangle's dark grip.

With a final, resolute glance at the central device, Evelyn and the crew stepped forward, ready to face whatever lay ahead. The Bermuda Triangle had revealed its path, and now they had to follow it, no matter where it might lead.

Chapter 13

The journey through the ship's labyrinthine corridors was marked by an oppressive silence. The eerie glow from the crystalline structure seemed to cast long, trembling shadows on the walls, amplifying the sense of dread that hung in the air. Evelyn led the way, her mind focused and her steps cautious. The symbols on the central device had shown a route, but navigating through the unknown was a daunting task.

As they advanced, the ship's environment seemed to change around them. The familiar walls gave way to unfamiliar, almost organic structures. The ship's architecture had become fluid, shifting and changing as if it were alive. The feeling of being watched grew stronger, a constant, unsettling presence that gnawed at their nerves.

The rhythmic pulsing of the central device resonated through the ship, guiding them with its haunting cadence. Evelyn could feel the vibration in her bones, a deep, unsettling hum that seemed to synchronize with the pounding of her heart. The air was charged with an almost palpable tension, and every sound seemed amplified in the oppressive silence.

"Do you see that?" Sarah's voice broke the silence, her tone filled with a mix of awe and fear.

Evelyn followed Sarah's gaze and saw a massive, swirling vortex ahead. The vortex was a swirling mass of darkness, its edges flickering with a sinister light. It seemed to draw everything toward it, a force of gravity that tugged at their very souls.

"That must be the heart of the Bermuda Triangle," Captain Harris said, his voice tight with apprehension. "It's the center of its power."

Evelyn nodded, her eyes fixed on the vortex. The closer they got, the more intense the sensation of being watched became. The air was thick with an almost tangible energy, a force that seemed to reach out and touch them with invisible hands. Evelyn's skin prickled, and she could feel a cold sweat forming on the back of her neck.

As they approached the vortex, the ship's corridor twisted and warped, the very space around them seeming to bend and stretch. The walls became indistinct, fading into the darkness that surrounded the vortex. The sense of disorientation was overwhelming, and Evelyn struggled to maintain her footing as the ship seemed to shift beneath them.

"We need to stay focused," Harris said, his voice steady despite the danger. "We're getting close."

The vortex's pull was strong, and Evelyn could feel it tugging at her, urging her to move faster. The rhythmic pulse of the central device grew more intense, its light flashing in time with the vortex's swirling darkness. The symbols on the device seemed to dance in the air, their glow merging with the vortex's ominous light.

Evelyn felt a surge of determination as she pressed forward. They had come too far to turn back now. The vortex was their final challenge, the last obstacle standing between them and escape. She could feel the weight of their journey pressing down on her, a burden of fear and hope that was almost too much to bear.

As they neared the vortex, the darkness seemed to envelop them, the ship's corridor vanishing into the swirling abyss. Evelyn could barely see the others, their figures becoming shadowy silhouettes against the encroaching darkness. The sense of isolation was overwhelming, and she felt as if she were drifting in a void.

"Hold on!" Harris's voice cut through the darkness, a beacon of resolve amidst the encroaching void. "We're almost there!"

With a final, determined effort, Evelyn and the crew moved forward, their path illuminated by the pulsating light of the central device. The vortex seemed to grow larger, its swirling darkness reaching out to consume them. Evelyn felt a strange pull, as if the vortex was trying to draw her into its depths.

As they reached the edge of the vortex, the central device emitted a brilliant flash of light, its rhythmic pulse creating a shield against the encroaching darkness. The light cut through the vortex, creating a narrow path that led deeper into the heart of the Triangle. Evelyn could see a faint glimmer of hope on the other side, a vision of freedom and escape that seemed just within reach.

"We need to go through," Evelyn said, her voice filled with determination. "It's our only chance."

Harris nodded, his expression resolute. "Let's move."

One by one, the crew stepped into the vortex, the darkness closing in around them. The pull of the vortex was intense, and Evelyn felt herself being dragged forward, her body feeling as if it were being stretched and compressed. The sensation was disorienting, and she struggled to maintain her focus as the darkness enveloped her.

The journey through the vortex seemed to stretch on forever, the darkness swirling around them in an endless, suffocating embrace. Evelyn could feel her senses becoming numb, her mind struggling to hold onto the fragments of reality. The rhythmic pulse of the central device was their only anchor, its light guiding them through the chaos.

Suddenly, the darkness gave way to a blinding flash of light. Evelyn felt a jolt, and the sensation of being pulled through the vortex abruptly stopped. She stumbled, her vision slowly clearing as the intense light faded. The corridor was gone, replaced by a vast, open space bathed in a soft, golden glow.

Evelyn looked around, her heart pounding with a mixture of relief and trepidation. They were in a new environment, one that was both beautiful and alien. The space was filled with an ethereal light, and the air was warm and soothing. The ground beneath them was covered in soft, glowing mist, and the sky above was a tapestry of swirling colors.

"We made it," Sarah said, her voice filled with awe.

"Yes," Evelyn replied, her voice trembling. "But where are we?"

The new environment was mesmerizing and disorienting. The ground seemed to shift beneath their feet, and the landscape was filled with strange, otherworldly formations. The air was filled with a soft, melodic hum, a soothing contrast to the oppressive darkness they had left behind.

"We need to find out where we are," Harris said, his voice steady despite the uncertainty. "And figure out how to get back home."

Evelyn nodded, her mind racing as she took in their surroundings. The new environment was unlike anything she had ever seen, and the sense of wonder was tinged with a deep sense of unease. The Bermuda Triangle had revealed its secrets, but the journey was far from over.

As they began to explore their new surroundings, Evelyn couldn't shake the feeling that they were not alone. The soft hum in the air seemed to be growing louder, and the glowing mist around them seemed to shimmer with an almost sentient energy. The beauty of the new environment was overshadowed by the sense of danger that lingered just beneath the surface.

"We need to stay together," Harris said, his voice firm. "We don't know what we might encounter."

Evelyn and the crew moved forward, their steps careful and deliberate. The new environment was both alien and mesmerizing, its beauty a stark contrast to the darkness they had just escaped. But the sense of unease remained, a constant reminder of the dangers that lay ahead.

As they ventured further into the strange, glowing landscape, Evelyn's thoughts were consumed by the mysteries of the Bermuda Triangle and the forces that controlled it. The journey had taken them to the heart of the Triangle, but the true nature of their surroundings was still shrouded in uncertainty.

With each step, Evelyn felt the weight of their journey pressing down on her. The Bermuda Triangle had revealed its secrets, but the path to freedom was still fraught with danger. They had to navigate through the unknown and confront whatever forces awaited them in this strange, new world.

As the crew continued their exploration, the sense of wonder and fear grew stronger. The new environment was both beautiful and terrifying, a reflection of the enigmatic power of the Bermuda Triangle. And as Evelyn looked toward the horizon, she knew that the journey was far from over.

Chapter 14

Evelyn's mind was awash with the surreal beauty of their new surroundings. The landscape stretched out before them, a vast expanse of iridescent mist and shifting colors that defied description. The air was filled with a melodic hum that seemed to resonate with an otherworldly rhythm. It was as though they had stepped into a realm that existed beyond the boundaries of their understanding a place where the rules of reality no longer applied.

The mist underfoot was soft and luminous, giving the impression of walking on a bed of clouds. Each step sent ripples through the mist, causing the ground to shimmer and shift. The sky above was a swirling tapestry of hues, with colors blending seamlessly into one another, creating an ever-changing panorama of light.

Evelyn glanced at her companions, Captain Harris, Sarah, and Collins who were equally awed and unsettled by their surroundings. The captain's usual stoic expression was replaced by a look of cautious wonder, while Sarah's face reflected a mix of awe and apprehension. Collins, on the other hand, seemed to be struggling with a sense of disbelief, his eyes darting nervously around.

"This place… it's incredible," Sarah said, her voice barely above a whisper. "But it feels like we're being watched."

Evelyn nodded, her own unease mirrored in Sarah's words. The sense of being observed was almost palpable, an unseen presence that seemed to linger just out of sight. Despite the ethereal beauty of their surroundings, the feeling of dread was impossible to ignore.

"We need to stay vigilant," Captain Harris said, his voice steady but filled with an edge of caution. "We don't know what kind of dangers might be lurking here."

The crew began to move forward, their steps tentative as they navigated the strange terrain. Evelyn took a deep breath, trying to steady her nerves. The rhythmic hum in the air seemed to grow louder, its melody both soothing and unsettling. It was as if the landscape itself was alive, resonating with an ancient and mysterious energy.

As they ventured deeper into the glowing expanse, Evelyn's thoughts turned to the symbols they had seen earlier. The patterns on the central device had shown a path, but the true nature of their destination remained unclear. They were in a new realm, one that seemed to exist outside the normal bounds of space and time.

Suddenly, a new feature of the landscape caught Evelyn's eye, a series of towering, crystalline formations that jutted up from the ground like jagged spires. The crystals glowed with an inner light, their surfaces covered in intricate patterns and symbols that seemed to pulse with a rhythmic energy.

"Look at those," Collins said, his voice filled with a mixture of awe and apprehension. "What are they?"

Evelyn approached the crystalline formations, her gaze drawn to the symbols etched into their surfaces. The patterns were like those on the central device, though they were more complex and intertwined. The symbols seemed to shimmer and shift, creating a mesmerizing, almost hypnotic effect.

"I think these crystals are connected to the energy we've been encountering," Evelyn said, her voice filled with a sense of wonder. "They might hold clues about this place and how we can navigate it."

As Evelyn examined the crystals, she felt a sudden, sharp tug in her chest a sensation that was both physical and emotional. It was as if the crystals were reaching out to her, trying to communicate something beyond words. The rhythmic hum in the air seemed to resonate with the crystals, creating a harmonious, yet eerie, symphony.

"I'm getting a strong reading from these crystals," Evelyn said, her voice filled with excitement. "They're definitely part of the same energy source. We need to find out what they're trying to tell us."

The crew gathered around the crystalline formations, their expressions a mix of curiosity and apprehension. The symbols on the crystals began to shift and change, forming new patterns that seemed to convey a message.

The message was fragmented and enigmatic, but it appeared to depict a journey a path through a series of challenges and trials. The symbols illustrated scenes of struggle and perseverance, of individuals facing immense obstacles and overcoming them through sheer will and determination.

"This is incredible," Sarah said, her eyes wide with wonder. "It's like a map of some kind, showing a path through the challenges we might face."

"Yes," Evelyn agreed, her mind racing with possibilities. "It looks like we're meant to follow this path, but it also seems to warn us about the dangers ahead."

The symbols on the crystals began to form a final, intricate pattern, a series of interconnected lines and shapes that seemed to converge on a central point. The pattern depicted a swirling vortex, like the one they had encountered earlier, but with additional symbols indicating a series of trials or tests.

"It looks like we're being guided through a series of trials," Evelyn said, her voice filled with a mixture of excitement and trepidation. "If we can navigate these trials, we might be able to reach the heart of this place and find a way out."

Harris nodded, his expression resolute. "Then we need to follow the path. We can't afford to turn back now."

With a renewed sense of purpose, the crew prepared to follow the path laid out by the crystals. The journey ahead was fraught with uncertainty, but the clues they had discovered provided a glimmer of hope. They had come too far to turn back, and the mysteries of the Bermuda Triangle were within their grasp.

As they set out along the path, the landscape shifted and changed around them. The soft, glowing mist seemed to swirl in response to their movements, creating a dynamic, ever-changing environment. The rhythmic hum in the air grew louder, its melody guiding them forward.

The trials depicted by the crystals seemed to come alive as they moved along the path. The landscape began to present challenges shifting terrain, treacherous obstacles, and strange, otherworldly phenomena that tested their resolve and adaptability. Each trial was a test of their strength and determination, pushing them to their limits.

Evelyn's heart raced as they navigated the trials, her mind focused on the patterns and symbols that guided them. The sense of being watched was ever-present, a constant reminder of the dark forces that lurked just beyond their perception. The trials were daunting, but Evelyn was determined to see them through.

As they faced each challenge, the crew worked together, their skills and teamwork becoming crucial to their survival. Captain Harris's leadership and experience were invaluable, while Sarah's keen observations and Collins's technical expertise provided essential support.

Despite the trials' difficulty, the crew pressed on, their resolve unwavering. Evelyn could feel the weight of their journey pressing down on her, a burden of fear and hope that was both exhilarating and exhausting. The path through the Bermuda Triangle was fraught with danger, but they were determined to uncover its secrets and find a way to escape.

With each trial they overcame, the path became clearer, guiding them toward the heart of the Bermuda Triangle. The journey was far from over, but the discoveries they had made provided a sense of purpose and hope. The mysteries of the Bermuda Triangle were within their reach, and Evelyn was determined to see it through to the end.

As they continued their journey, the landscape seemed to shift and change, revealing new challenges and opportunities. The path was treacherous, but the crew's determination and teamwork kept them moving forward. The heart of the Bermuda Triangle awaited them, and they were ready to face whatever lay ahead.

Chapter 15

As Evelyn and her team pressed on through the surreal landscape, the trials grew increasingly intricate and formidable. The ground beneath their feet was no longer a soft, glowing mist but a shifting, semi-solid surface that seemed to pulse with a life of its own. It undulated like a living organism, occasionally giving way beneath them, forcing them to scramble for balance.

The sky above had morphed into a swirling vortex of color, with hues that seemed to defy the spectrum of visible light. Occasionally, fleeting images of distant, unknown realms flickered in and out of view amidst the swirling chaos, adding to the disorienting effect. Evelyn's senses were overwhelmed, her perception stretched to its limits by the strange and unending stimuli.

"Stay close," Captain Harris instructed, his voice resonating with authority. "We need to keep our wits about us."

Evelyn nodded, though her focus was divided between maintaining her footing and deciphering the symbols that continued to appear around them. Each trial presented new patterns, complex, shifting geometries that seemed to be both a map and a warning. The symbols often seemed to change as she approached, making it difficult to determine their exact meaning.

As they navigated through the shifting terrain, Evelyn's thoughts were a whirlwind of concern and determination. The oppressive sense of being observed had intensified, a shadow that seemed to loom over their every move. It was as though some unseen force was scrutinizing their progress, a spectral presence that both intrigued and terrified her.

The rhythmic hum of the crystals had become an almost tangible sensation, vibrating through the ground and the air. The sound was both a guide and a tormentor, its melodic cadence resonating with a haunting beauty that was as alluring as it was unsettling.

"Is it just me," Sarah said, her voice tinged with anxiety, "Or does it feel like the ground is... alive?"

Evelyn glanced at Sarah, seeing the unease in her eyes. "It's not just you. Everything here seems to have a kind of sentience. It's like the landscape is reacting to us."

Collins, who had been unusually quiet, finally spoke up, his voice strained. "I keep feeling like there's something just beyond the edge of my vision. Like it's waiting for us to make a mistake."

Evelyn shared his concern. The feeling was almost primal, a deep-seated dread that seemed to tap into their most fundamental fears. It was as if the Bermuda Triangle itself was alive, its consciousness probing their every thought and action.

The next trial they encountered was a massive chasm that yawned open in the ground, its depths obscured by a swirling mist that seemed to reach out and beckon them forward. The edges of the chasm were lined with strange, glowing runes that pulsed with a rhythmic energy, and the very air around it felt heavy with anticipation.

"This must be one of the final trials," Evelyn said, her voice steady despite the anxiety gnawing at her insides. "We have to get across."

Captain Harris assessed the situation, his gaze scanning the chasm and the runes that surrounded it. "We'll need to find a way to traverse this. Look for any clues or mechanisms that might help us."

As the crew began to search for a solution, Evelyn found herself drawn to the runes on the chasm's edge. The symbols were intricate, their patterns reminiscent of those they had seen on the crystalline formations. They seemed to be a part of a larger puzzle, a final piece of the enigma they needed to solve.

Evelyn reached out and touched one of the runes, her fingers brushing against its cool, smooth surface. The moment she made contact, the rune began to glow with a soft, pulsing light. The chasm seemed to respond to the rune, its edges stabilizing and forming a narrow, glowing bridge that spanned the gap.

"That might be our way across," Evelyn said, her voice filled with cautious optimism. "But we need to be careful. We don't know what else might be waiting for us."

The crew began to carefully make their way across the glowing bridge, each step taken with deliberate caution. The bridge seemed to hum with energy, its surface vibrating slightly as they moved. Evelyn could feel the pulse of the runes beneath her feet, a rhythmic sensation that guided them forward.

As they reached the other side, the bridge dissipated, its light fading into the surrounding mist. The chasm was now behind them, but the sense of foreboding remained. The landscape ahead was shrouded in a dense fog, its outlines obscured by an impenetrable darkness.

The fog was thick and heavy, swirling around them like a living entity. It was difficult to see more than a few feet ahead, and the air was filled with a dense, oppressive silence. Evelyn could feel her heart pounding in her chest, each beat echoing in the stillness.

"We need to keep moving," Captain Harris said, his voice firm and reassuring. "This fog won't last forever."

The crew pressed forward into the fog, their senses on high alert. The darkness seemed to close in around them, and the rhythmic hum of the crystals became a distant echo. The feeling of being watched grew more intense, and Evelyn could feel a shiver running down her spine.

"Stay close and watch your step," Evelyn instructed, her voice barely audible above the heavy silence.

As they moved through the fog, the landscape began to shift again, revealing new features that seemed both alien and familiar. Strange, luminescent plants emerged from the mist, their tendrils swaying gently in an unseen breeze. The plants emitted a soft, soothing glow, their light creating eerie shadows on the surrounding fog.

Evelyn reached out and touched one of the plants, its surface cool and smooth. The moment she made contact, the fog began to thin, revealing a large, circular platform ahead. The platform was surrounded by more of the crystalline formations they had seen earlier, and at its center stood a towering obelisk, its surface covered in glowing runes.

"This must be it," Evelyn said, her voice filled with a mixture of relief and trepidation. "We've reached the heart of the Bermuda Triangle."

The obelisk's runes seemed to pulse with a rhythmic energy, their light growing brighter as they approached. The symbols on the obelisk were more complex and intricate than any they had seen before, their patterns forming a labyrinthine network of shapes and lines.

"This is incredible," Sarah said, her voice filled with awe. "It's like the culmination of everything we've encountered."

Evelyn nodded, her mind racing as she studied the obelisk. The symbols seemed to be a key, a final piece of the puzzle that would unlock the secrets of the Bermuda Triangle. The rhythmic hum in the air grew louder, its melody resonating with the obelisk's runes.

"We need to decipher these symbols," Evelyn said, her voice steady despite the weight of their situation. "They hold the key to our escape."

The crew gathered around the obelisk; their eyes focused on the glowing runes. Evelyn could feel the weight of their journey pressing down on her, a burden of fear and hope that was both exhilarating and exhausting. The Bermuda Triangle had revealed its secrets, but the true challenge was still ahead.

As Evelyn and her team worked to decipher the runes, the sense of anticipation grew stronger. The obelisk seemed to hold the answers they sought, but unlocking its secrets would require every ounce of their skill and determination.

The fog around them began to clear, and the platform was bathed in the soft, golden light of dawn. The first light of morning pierced through the mist, illuminating the landscape with a warm, ethereal glow. It was a beautiful and serene moment, a stark contrast to the trials they had endured.

Evelyn took a deep breath, her heart filled with a mix of hope and apprehension. The journey was far from over, but they were closer than ever to uncovering the mysteries of the Bermuda Triangle. The path to freedom was within their reach, and she was determined to see it through to the end.

With renewed resolve, Evelyn and the crew continued their efforts, their eyes fixed on the towering obelisk and the secrets it held. The Bermuda Triangle had revealed its heart, and now they had to unlock its mysteries and find a way to escape.

Chapter 16

As Evelyn and her team stood before the towering obelisk, the dawning light began to cast long, dramatic shadows across the circular platform. The soft, golden hue of morning light was a surreal contrast to the oppressive darkness they had just traversed. The intricate symbols on the obelisk glowed with an intense, pulsating light, their patterns shifting and intertwining in a mesmerizing dance.

The team was silent, each member absorbed in their own thoughts and feelings. The weight of their journey hung heavily in the air, mingling with the anticipation of what lay ahead. Evelyn could feel the tension in her muscles, the lingering ache of the trials they had endured. Her mind was a storm of emotions hope, fear, and an intense curiosity that drove her forward.

"We need to figure out how to interact with these symbols," Evelyn said, her voice steady but laced with a sense of urgency. She reached out and touched one of the glowing runes. The moment her fingers made contact, a shiver ran through her, as if the very essence of the obelisk was resonating with her touch.

As Evelyn explored the runes, she could feel an almost imperceptible vibration emanating from them. The symbols seemed to respond to her presence, their light growing brighter and their patterns shifting in a rhythmic, almost hypnotic manner. She tried to decipher the symbols, recalling the patterns she had seen on the crystalline formations and the central device.

"It's like they're alive," Sarah said, her voice filled with awe and trepidation. "The runes seem to be reacting to our presence."

Evelyn nodded, her focus unwavering as she studied the obelisk. "It's as if they're trying to communicate with us. We need to understand what they're saying."

Captain Harris was pacing around the platform, his eyes scanning the surroundings for any additional clues. "If these symbols are meant to guide us, there must be a way to interpret them. We need to find the key."

As Evelyn continued her examination, she felt an increasing sense of urgency. The rhythmic hum of the crystals had become almost deafening, its melody resonating with an intense, almost oppressive force. It was as if the obelisk was trying to convey a message through the vibrations and light.

Collins, who had been unusually quiet, suddenly spoke up, his voice trembling with excitement. "I think I've seen these symbols before. They resemble ancient markings from a civilization that supposedly disappeared thousands of years ago."

Evelyn's heart raced as she considered Collins's words. "Are you saying that these symbols are connected to an ancient civilization? That would mean we're on the brink of discovering something monumental."

"Yes," Collins replied, his eyes wide with anticipation. "These markings were believed to be a form of communication, a way to connect with forces beyond our understanding. If we can decipher them, we might unlock the secrets of this place."

The team's excitement was palpable, but so was the underlying sense of danger. The obelisk's light seemed to pulse with a growing intensity, and the rhythmic hum became more insistent. The platform beneath them began to tremble slightly, as if reacting to their discovery.

"Stay focused," Captain Harris said, his voice firm. "We need to be careful. We don't know what might happen if we disturb the balance."

Evelyn took a deep breath and concentrated on the symbols. She traced the intricate patterns with her fingers, trying to match them with the symbols they had seen before. The obelisk seemed to respond to her touch, its light fluctuating and creating a series of shifting images that played out before her eyes.

The images depicted scenes of ancient rituals and celestial alignments, a cosmic dance that seemed to transcend time and space. The symbols told a story of an advanced civilization that had harnessed the power of the Bermuda Triangle, using it to explore the boundaries of reality and unlock the secrets of the universe.

"This is incredible," Evelyn said, her voice filled with a mixture of awe and disbelief. "It's like we're witnessing the history of this place, the very foundation of its power."

As Evelyn continued to study the obelisk, the air around them grew colder, and a dense, oppressive fog began to swirl around the platform. The fog seemed to pulse with an eerie energy, its tendrils reaching out and enveloping the team in a shroud of darkness.

"What's happening?" Sarah asked, her voice tinged with fear. "Why is the fog returning?"

"It must be a reaction to our interaction with the obelisk," Evelyn said, her voice steady but filled with concern. "We need to be cautious. The fog could be a manifestation of the power we're tapping into."

The fog thickened, and the platform began to tremble more violently. The glowing runes on the obelisk flickered erratically, their light casting eerie, distorted shadows on the surrounding mist. The rhythmic hum of the crystals grew louder, creating a cacophony of sound that reverberated through the air.

Evelyn could feel the pressure building, the weight of their actions pressing down on her. The sense of being watched had become almost overwhelming, a spectral presence that seemed to loom over them with malevolent intent.

"We need to finish this quickly," Captain Harris said, his voice tight with urgency. "If the fog is a response to our actions, we need to complete the process before it's too late."

Evelyn nodded, her mind racing as she worked to decipher the final patterns on the obelisk. The symbols were becoming clearer, their meaning revealing itself in a series of interconnected lines and shapes. It was a complex puzzle, but Evelyn's determination kept her focused.

As she completed the final sequence, the obelisk's light erupted in a blinding flash, momentarily illuminating the entire platform. The fog dissipated rapidly, swirling away and revealing a new, previously hidden feature of the landscape.

Before them stood a massive, ancient gate, its surface covered in the same glowing runes as the obelisk. The gate was ornate and imposing, its structure seemingly carved from a single piece of luminous crystal. It radiated a sense of both grandeur and foreboding.

"This must be the way forward," Evelyn said, her voice filled with awe and determination. "The gate is our path to the next phase of the journey."

The team approached the gate, their steps echoing with a sense of purpose. The runes on the gate glowed with a steady, inviting light, and the air around it was filled with a serene, almost calming energy.

Evelyn reached out and touched the gate, her fingers brushing against the smooth, cool surface. The moment she made contact, the gate began to slowly open, its massive doors sliding apart with a soft, resonant hum.

Beyond the gate lay a vast chamber, its interior bathed in a soft, golden light. The chamber was filled with ancient artifacts and celestial maps, their surfaces covered in intricate symbols and patterns. It was a place of profound beauty and mystery, a repository of knowledge and power.

"This is it," Evelyn said, her voice filled with a mixture of relief and excitement. "We've reached the heart of the Bermuda Triangle."

As the team stepped into the chamber, they were enveloped by a sense of awe and reverence. The ancient artifacts and maps spoke of a civilization that had mastered the forces of the universe, harnessing the power of the Bermuda Triangle to explore the limits of reality.

Evelyn's heart raced as she took in the chamber's wonders. The discoveries they had made were beyond anything she had ever imagined, and the journey was far from over. The secrets of the Bermuda Triangle were within their grasp, but the true challenge was still ahead.

With renewed determination, Evelyn and her team prepared to explore the chamber and unlock the final mysteries of their journey. The heart of the Bermuda Triangle awaited them, and they were ready to face whatever lay beyond.

Chapter 17

Evelyn stepped through the ancient gate into the vast chamber, her heart pounding with a mixture of awe and trepidation. The chamber was illuminated by a soft, golden light that seemed to emanate from the very walls, casting a warm, almost celestial glow across the room. The space was vast, with high, vaulted ceilings and an intricate network of arches and pillars that supported the structure.

The air was filled with a palpable sense of reverence, and the soft hum of the obelisk's energy seemed to resonate through the chamber, creating a harmonious, soothing melody. The artifacts and celestial maps that filled the room were arranged with meticulous care, their surfaces covered in a myriad of symbols and patterns that spoke of a profound and ancient knowledge.

Evelyn's breath caught in her throat as she took in the sight before her. The chamber was a repository of secrets, a hidden trove of wisdom from a civilization that had transcended the boundaries of ordinary understanding. Her mind raced with possibilities, her thoughts a whirlwind of excitement and apprehension.

"It's... beautiful," Sarah whispered, her voice filled with wonder. She moved closer to a celestial map, her fingers hovering over the intricate patterns that adorned its surface.

Collins was equally entranced, his eyes wide with amazement as he examined a series of ancient artifacts—crystal orbs and metal devices arranged on stone pedestals. "This is like nothing I've ever seen. It's as if we've stepped into the heart of an ancient civilization's most sacred knowledge."

Captain Harris, ever the pragmatic leader, was carefully observing the chamber's layout and the potential implications of their discovery. "We need to be cautious. There's no telling what kind of forces or mechanisms might be at play here."

Evelyn nodded, her own sense of wonder tempered by the need for vigilance. As she moved further into the chamber, she felt a deep, almost primal connection to the artifacts and symbols that surrounded her. The feeling was both exhilarating and unnerving, as if she were on the brink of uncovering truths that could fundamentally alter her understanding of the world.

She approached one of the celestial maps, its surface covered in a complex network of lines and symbols that seemed to chart the movements of celestial bodies and the flow of cosmic energies. The map was mesmerizing, its intricate details creating a sense of awe and reverence.

As Evelyn studied the map, she could feel a subtle shift in the chamber's atmosphere. The air grew cooler, and the golden light seemed to dim slightly. The rhythmic hum of the obelisk's energy became more intense, its melody resonating with a sense of urgency.

"This map," Evelyn said, her voice trembling slightly with excitement, "it's showing the alignments of stars and planets. It's like a guide to understanding the cosmic forces that shape our reality."

Captain Harris moved closer, his expression a mix of curiosity and caution. "If this map is as detailed as it seems, it might provide us with the key to understanding the Bermuda Triangle's mysteries."

Collins was examining a nearby pedestal, his fingers tracing the contours of a crystal orb. "This orb could be a tool for harnessing or measuring cosmic energy. If we can figure out how it works, it might help us unlock the chamber's secrets."

Evelyn's thoughts were a storm of excitement and apprehension. The discoveries they were making were staggering, but the sense of being watched, the feeling of unseen forces lurking just beyond their perception, was ever-present. It was as though the very chamber itself was alive, its energy resonating with a consciousness that was both ancient and profound.

As they continued their exploration, Evelyn's gaze was drawn to a central altar at the heart of the chamber. The altar was adorned with intricate symbols and inlaid with precious stones that glowed with an inner light. At its center was a large, crystallized object that seemed to pulse with a rhythmic energy, its surface covered in more of the enigmatic runes they had encountered throughout their journey.

"This must be the focal point of the chamber," Evelyn said, her voice filled with reverence. "The central artifact might hold the key to understanding the energy we've been encountering."

The team gathered around the altar, their expressions a mix of awe and determination. Evelyn reached out and touched the central crystal, her fingers brushing against its cool, smooth surface. The moment she made contact, a surge of energy flowed through her, sending a jolt of sensation through her entire body.

The chamber was suddenly filled with a blinding light, its intensity overwhelming. Evelyn shielded her eyes, her heart racing as the light seemed to pierce through the very fabric of reality. The symbols on the crystal and the altar began to glow with a brilliant, pulsating light, their patterns shifting and intertwining in a mesmerizing dance.

As the light began to fade, Evelyn could see that the chamber had transformed. The walls and floor were now covered in a shimmering, translucent membrane that seemed to pulse with a rhythmic energy. The celestial maps and artifacts were gone, replaced by a vast, swirling vortex of light and color that filled the space.

"What's happening?" Sarah's voice was filled with a mixture of fear and wonder.

"I don't know," Evelyn said, her voice trembling with awe. "But it looks like we're about to uncover something truly extraordinary."

The vortex seemed to be drawing them in, its swirling energies creating a sense of both exhilaration and trepidation. The rhythmic hum of the obelisk's energy had become a resonant, almost symphonic melody, guiding them through the swirling vortex.

Evelyn's mind was a whirlwind of thoughts and emotions. The journey had brought them to the heart of the Bermuda Triangle, and now they were on the brink of discovering the ultimate truth. The chamber's transformation was both awe-inspiring and disorienting, a profound shift that defied their understanding.

As they moved through the vortex, the swirling colors and lights began to coalesce into a series of images and symbols. It was as if the very fabric of reality was unravelling, revealing the hidden truths of the universe. The images depicted scenes of cosmic events, ancient rituals, and celestial alignments, an intricate tapestry of knowledge that spanned the ages.

Evelyn could feel the energy of the vortex enveloping her, its rhythmic pulse resonating with her own heartbeat. The experience was both exhilarating and overwhelming, a profound connection to forces that transcended their understanding.

"Hold on," Captain Harris's voice cut through the swirling chaos. "We need to stay together."

The team gripped each other's hands, their resolve unwavering as they moved through the vortex. The swirling colors and lights seemed to create a path, guiding them toward a central point of convergence.

As they reached the center of the vortex, the energy began to coalesce into a single, radiant point of light. The light was blinding, its intensity overwhelming, but it also held a sense of profound clarity and understanding. Evelyn could feel the very essence of the universe converging on this single point, revealing the secrets of the Bermuda Triangle.

The light began to fade, and the vortex slowly dissipated. Evelyn and her team found themselves standing in a new, serene landscape an ethereal realm that seemed to exist outside the bounds of time and space. The air was filled with a soothing, harmonic resonance, and the surroundings were bathed in a soft, golden glow.

Evelyn looked around, her heart filled with a sense of wonder and accomplishment. The journey had led them to the heart of the Bermuda Triangle, and they had uncovered truths that transcended ordinary understanding. The mysteries of the Triangle had been revealed, and the ultimate revelation was within their grasp.

The team stood in silence, their expressions a mix of awe and reverence. The journey had been arduous, but the discoveries they had made were nothing short of extraordinary. The secrets of the Bermuda Triangle had been unveiled, and the path forward was now clear.

Evelyn took a deep breath, her heart filled with a profound sense of fulfillment. The journey had been one of discovery and enlightenment, a journey that had revealed the hidden truths of the universe. As they prepared to explore this new realm, Evelyn was filled with a sense of hope and anticipation for what lay ahead.

Chapter 18

The new realm that Evelyn and her team had entered was nothing short of awe-inspiring, yet as they ventured further, the atmosphere became increasingly unsettling. The ethereal beauty of the floating islands and crystalline structures was undeniable, but there was a disquieting undercurrent, a sense that they had crossed into a place not meant for human eyes. The soft, golden light that bathed the landscape seemed to pulsate with a rhythm that was almost hypnotic, but the rhythm was off, just slightly, enough to make Evelyn's skin prickle.

Evelyn's thoughts churned with the weight of their discovery. She had anticipated many things about this expedition danger, uncertainty, the potential for groundbreaking revelations, but this, this surreal blend of beauty and menace, was beyond anything she could have prepared for. She could sense the others were feeling it too, though they said nothing. Sarah's wide eyes darted nervously, and Collins' normally unflappable demeanor had given way to a furrowed brow and tight jaw.

"This place is... alive," Collins finally murmured, his voice barely audible over the soft hum that permeated the air. He glanced at Evelyn, his expression a mixture of wonder and concern. "It's like it's aware of us, reacting to us."

Evelyn nodded, her own unease growing. The idea that the realm could be conscious, or at least responsive in some way, was both fascinating and terrifying. Her mind raced through the implications if the realm was reacting to them, then their actions might have far-reaching consequences, beyond anything they could predict. And yet, they had no choice but to press on. The answers they sought lay ahead, and turning back now was unthinkable.

Captain Harris was already moving forward, his military instincts overriding any hesitation. "We need to keep moving," he said, his tone firm but laced with a subtle edge of tension. "We don't know how stable this place is. We should get to that structure and figure out what we're dealing with."

The others followed his lead, but Evelyn lingered for a moment, taking in the shifting landscape. The floating islands, which had seemed so serene at first, were now drifting with an almost imperceptible unease, as if they were alive and could sense the disturbance their presence had caused. The crystalline formations emitted a soft, pulsating glow, but the light flickered now, as if in response to some unseen force.

Evelyn's heart pounded as she hurried to catch up with the group, the sense of being watched growing stronger with each step. The atmosphere felt heavier, as though the very air was thick with unseen eyes and whispered warnings. The serenity of the realm had become a fragile veneer, barely concealing the turmoil that lurked beneath the surface.

As they approached the towering spire of crystal, Evelyn felt a strange pull, an almost magnetic attraction to the structure. The symbols etched into its surface glowed with an intensity that made her breath catch in her throat. They were more than just markings they were alive, shifting and changing as if communicating with the team, or perhaps with the realm itself.

"This spire… it's not just a structure," Evelyn murmured, her fingers hovering over the glowing symbols. "It's a conduit, a nexus of the energy that flows through this entire realm. If we can understand it, maybe we can figure out how to stabilize whatever's happening here."

But as she reached out to touch the spire, the ground beneath them began to tremble. The tremors were subtle at first, like the gentle shaking of a leaf in the wind, but quickly grew more violent, the ground rippling as if it were a living thing in distress. The spire's light intensified, bathing them in a blinding glow that made Evelyn's head spin.

"What the hell is happening?" Sarah gasped; her voice high with panic as the ground lurched beneath her feet.

Evelyn pulled her hand back, her heart hammering in her chest. "I think... I think we've triggered something. The realm is reacting to us, but I don't know if it's a defense mechanism or something else."

Before they could speculate further, the serene beauty of the realm shattered like glass. The crystalline structures that had seemed so solid and eternal began to crack and splinter, the sound echoing like the shattering of ice. The floating islands, once graceful and serene, began to drift erratically, crashing into one another with deafening booms that reverberated through the air.

The melodic hum that had filled the air shifted into a discordant, almost malevolent tone. The very fabric of the realm seemed to twist and writhe, as if in agony. The sky, if it could be called that, darkened, the soft twilight giving way to swirling, inky blackness shot through with jagged streaks of crimson lightning.

"Evelyn!" Captain Harris shouted, his voice barely audible over the cacophony of destruction. "We need to move, now!"

But Evelyn was rooted to the spot, her mind racing as she tried to make sense of what was happening. She could feel the realm's pain, its confusion, as if it were a living entity struggling against forces beyond its control. And she realized, with a cold, sinking feeling, that they were the cause. Their presence, their actions, had disrupted the delicate balance of this

place.

"We've… we've broken something," Evelyn whispered, her voice trembling with the weight of the realization. "This realm… it's reacting to us because we've upset the balance. We need to find a way to fix it, or we're all going to be trapped here, or worse."

But before she could act, the tremors intensified, and the ground beneath them split open with a deafening crack. The team was thrown to the ground as the earth heaved and buckled, and a gaping chasm yawned before them, its depths shrouded in impenetrable darkness. From within the chasm, a cold wind began to blow, carrying with it a sound that made Evelyn's blood run cold, a low, mournful wail, like the cry of a wounded animal or the lament of a lost soul.

And then, from the darkness of the chasm, the figure emerged. It was the same shadowy figure they had seen earlier, but now it was fully formed, a towering, menacing presence that radiated malice. Its eyes, if they could be called that, glowed with a sickly, unnatural light, and its form seemed to shift and flicker, as if it were not entirely bound by the laws of reality.

"Who are you?" Evelyn demanded, her voice trembling with both fear and defiance. "What do you want from us?"

The figure's eyes locked onto hers, and she felt a wave of cold dread wash over her. When it spoke, its voice was a low, rasping whisper that seemed to reverberate inside her skull.

"You have trespassed into a realm not meant for the living," it hissed, its voice filled with ancient anger. "The balance has been broken, and now you must pay the price."

Evelyn's mind raced as she tried to comprehend what the figure was saying. The realm's turmoil, the sudden chaos—they were all consequences of their intrusion. But there was something else, something deeper and more sinister at play.

"What do you mean?" Evelyn asked, her voice barely above a whisper. "What price?"

The figure raised a shadowy hand, and the chasm beneath them began to widen, its depths swirling with darkness and an ominous red glow. "The balance must be restored," it intoned. "One must be sacrificed to close the rift, to heal the wound you have inflicted upon this realm."

Evelyn's heart skipped a beat, the horror of the situation sinking in. One of them had to stay behind, to become part of this alien realm, in order to set things right. The very thought was terrifying, but the figure's presence left no room for doubt, it was deadly serious.

The others exchanged fearful glances, the weight of the figure's words settling over them like a suffocating blanket. Evelyn could see the fear in their eyes, but also a grim determination. They had come this far, and they knew that if they didn't act, none of them would make it out alive.

"No!" Sarah cried, shaking her head furiously. "There must be another way! We can't just…."

"We don't have a choice," Captain Harris interrupted, his voice steady but filled with grim resolve. "We have to do what's necessary to save the others."

Evelyn's mind raced. She couldn't ask any of them to make such a sacrifice, but at the same time, she knew that one of them had to. The figure's demand was clear, and the turmoil of the realm was growing more intense by the second. The ground continued to quake, the air thick with the acrid scent of ozone and something far more ancient, something primal and terrifying.

But then, something clicked in Evelyn's mind, a realization that sent a jolt of both hope and fear through her. The figure had said the balance must be restored, that one must be sacrificed to heal the wound. But it hadn't said that the sacrifice had to be human.

Her gaze snapped to the spire, its surface still glowing with the enigmatic symbols that had seemed to resonate with their presence. What if the spire itself could be the key to restoring the balance? What if they could channel the energy they had unleashed back into the spire, using it as a conduit to heal the realm?

"It doesn't have to be one of us!" Evelyn shouted, her voice cutting through the chaos. "The spire, if we can channel the energy into it, we might be able to restore the balance without losing anyone!"

The figure's eyes narrowed, its form flickering as if in surprise. But it made no move to stop them.

"Are you sure?" Collins asked, his voice filled with both hope and doubt. "What if it doesn't work?"

Evelyn met his gaze, her own eyes filled with steely determination. "It's a risk, but it's the only chance we've got. We can't just give up now. We must try."

Without waiting for further debate, she reached out to the spire, her hands trembling as she pressed them against its cool, glowing surface. The symbols flared brighter, and she could feel a surge of energy coursing through her, a connection that resonated deep within her very being.

"Focus!" she shouted to the others; her voice filled with urgency. "We need to channel everything we've got into the spire. It's the only way!"

The others hesitated only for a moment before following her lead, each of them placing their hands on the spire, their faces set with determination. The air around them crackled with energy, and the ground beneath them began to steady as they focused their combined will into the spire.

For a moment, nothing happened. The realm's chaos continued to swirl around them, the figure looming ominously, its presence a constant reminder of the stakes. But then, slowly, the spire began to pulse with a deep, rhythmic glow, the light spreading outwards like ripples on a pond.

The figure's eyes widened, its form flickering as if in distress. "What are you doing?" it demanded, its voice filled with anger and fear.

"We're restoring the balance," Evelyn replied, her voice strong and resolute. "We're not giving up without a fight."

The light from the spire continued to spread, enveloping the landscape in a soft, warm glow. The chaotic forces that had threatened to tear the realm apart began to dissipate, the ground steadying beneath their feet. The dark clouds overhead parted, revealing a clear, star-filled sky that seemed to stretch on forever. Evelyn could feel the energy of the realm flowing through her, a connection that went beyond the physical, reaching into the very essence of her being. She could feel the pain of the realm, its confusion and fear, but also its hope, its desire for balance and harmony. And she knew, with absolute certainty, that they were doing the right thing.

The figure let out a howl of rage, its form dissolving into shadow as the light from the spire intensified. The chasm that had threatened to consume them began to close, the darkness receding as the realm began to heal itself. The ground beneath them solidified, the tremors ceasing as the energy they had channeled into the spire was absorbed, restoring the balance that had been disrupted.

As the last of the darkness faded, Evelyn felt a sense of profound relief wash over her. They had done it—they had restored the balance without losing anyone. The figure was gone, the realm was calm, and the spire's light had returned to its soft, steady glow.

But as the adrenaline began to fade, she realized how exhausted she was, her body trembling with the effort it had taken to channel the energy. The others were in a similar state, their faces pale and drawn, but there was a sense of triumph in their eyes, a shared knowledge that they had faced the impossible and emerged victorious.

"We did it," Sarah whispered, her voice filled with awe and disbelief. "I can't believe we actually did it."

Evelyn smiled, her heart swelling with pride and relief. "We did," she agreed, her voice barely above a whisper. "We saved the realm, and ourselves."

But as they began to collect themselves, preparing to find a way back home, Evelyn couldn't shake the feeling that something was still not quite right. The realm was calm, the balance restored, but there was a lingering sense of unease, a nagging doubt that refused to be silenced.

And then, as if in response to her thoughts, the spire began to pulse with light once more. The symbols on its surface shifted, rearranging themselves into a new pattern, one that Evelyn recognized with a jolt of fear.

It was a map.

A map that led deeper into the realm, to a place they had not yet discovered.

The realization hit her like a cold wave. Their journey wasn't over. The balance had been restored, but the mystery of the Bermuda Triangle had only deepened. There were still answers to be found, and dangers to be faced.

As she gazed at the glowing map, Evelyn knew that they had no choice but to continue. The realm had revealed its secrets to them, but it had also shown them that there was much more at stake than they had ever imagined.

"We're not done yet," she said, her voice filled with both dread and determination. "There's more to this realm, more that we need to uncover. And we must keep going."

The others looked at her, their faces reflecting the same mixture of fear and resolve. They had come too far to turn back now. The mysteries of the Bermuda Triangle were waiting, and they were the only ones who could uncover the truth.

With a deep breath, Evelyn turned towards the new path that had been revealed, the light from the spire guiding them forward. The journey ahead would be even more dangerous, even more challenging, but she was ready to face whatever lay ahead.

They had restored the balance, but the true test was only just beginning.

Chapter 19

The air in the mysterious realm was thick with anticipation, almost as if the place itself was holding its breath. The map that had emerged on the spire's surface pulsed with a steady rhythm, its light casting long, shifting shadows on the faces of Evelyn and her team. The initial triumph of restoring balance had been replaced by a heavy silence, each member of the group lost in their own thoughts, grappling with the realization that their journey was far from over.

Evelyn stared at the map, her heart a mix of dread and determination. The path it outlined was clear, leading them deeper into this otherworldly place, towards a destination shrouded in mystery. She couldn't shake the feeling that this next step would be even more dangerous than anything they had faced so far.

"We don't have to do this," Sarah said suddenly, her voice trembling. She hugged herself tightly, her eyes wide with fear. "We've already accomplished so much. Maybe we should just find a way back, while we still can."

Evelyn turned to her, understanding the fear that gripped her friend. Sarah's normally bright and confident demeanor had cracked under the weight of their experiences. Evelyn could see the exhaustion in her eyes, the strain of holding herself together through everything they had endured.

"I know how you feel, Sarah," Evelyn replied, her voice gentle. "But there's something we haven't uncovered yet, something that could be crucial. We can't leave without knowing what it is. We need to understand what's really going on here, not just for us, but for everyone who's ever been lost to this place."

Collins nodded in agreement, though his expression was grim. The lines on his face seemed deeper now, etched by the fear and tension that had been building since they first entered the Triangle. "Evelyn's right," he said quietly. "We're so close to the truth. If we walk away now, we'll never forgive ourselves. We need to finish this."

Captain Harris, who had been silent until now, stepped forward. His eyes, usually so calm and calculating, held a new intensity. "We have a duty to see this through," he said firmly. "This place, whatever it is, has taken too many lives. If there's even a chance, we can put an end to that, we must take it." The captain's words, though resolute, were not without their own undercurrent of emotion. He was a man used to being in control, to understanding the terrain he was navigating. But here, in this alien realm, the rules were different, the dangers unknowable. The fear of the unknown gnawed at him, but he kept it tightly controlled, buried beneath the surface.

Evelyn could see the determination in his stance, the way he squared his shoulders as if preparing to lead his team into battle. But she could also see the subtle tension in his jaw, the way his hands clenched at his sides. He was as afraid as the rest of them, but he would never show it.

"We do this together," Evelyn said, trying to muster her own courage and infuse her words with confidence. "We've made it this far because we've relied on each other. Whatever happens next, we face it as a team."

The others nodded, though the fear in their eyes didn't completely fade. They were all aware that the path ahead was fraught with danger, but Evelyn's words had sparked a renewed sense of unity among them. Whatever they faced, they would face it together.

As they turned to follow the map's path, the landscape around them began to shift. The floating islands, once so distant and isolated, started to drift closer, forming a winding trail that led them deeper into the heart of the realm. The light from the spire illuminated the way, casting an eerie glow over the jagged rocks and strange vegetation that seemed to pulse with its own life.

Evelyn led the way, her eyes fixed on the map that hovered before her. The symbols on the spire continued to shift and change, guiding them with a certainty that was both reassuring and unsettling. She couldn't shake the feeling that they were being watched that the realm itself was aware of their every move.

Her mind raced with questions. What was the true nature of this place? Was it a creation of some advanced civilization, a natural phenomenon, or something else entirely? And why had it taken so many lives over the centuries, only to now reveal itself to them?

The silence was heavy, broken only by the occasional sound of their footsteps on the rocky ground. Each member of the team was lost in their own thoughts, processing the events that had brought them to this point. Sarah, usually so vibrant and full of life, was subdued, her eyes darting nervously around as if expecting danger to leap out at any moment. She stayed close to Evelyn, as if drawing strength from her friend's presence.

"I can't stop thinking about all those people who vanished here," Sarah said softly, breaking the silence. "What happened to them? Are they… could they still be here, somewhere?"

Evelyn felt a chill run down her spine at the thought. The idea that the missing might still be trapped in this realm, caught between worlds, was a terrifying one. "I don't know," she admitted, her voice tinged with sadness. "But if they are, maybe we can find a way to help them."

Sarah nodded, though her expression remained troubled. She had always been the optimist of the group, the one who believed in the best possible outcome. But this place had shaken her faith, and Evelyn could see the doubt in her eyes.

Collins, who had been walking in silence beside them, suddenly spoke up. "I keep thinking about that figure," he said, his voice low and thoughtful. "The way it reacted when we restored the balance... it seemed almost afraid. What if it wasn't just trying to stop us? What if it was trying to protect something?"

Evelyn frowned, considering his words. The figure's anger had been palpable, but there had also been a sense of desperation, as if it was fighting to preserve something vital. "You might be right," she said slowly. "This realm... it's more than just a trap. There's something deeper going on here, something that figure was willing to fight to protect." Captain Harris, who had been listening quietly, glanced over at them. "If that's true, then whatever we're heading towards could be even more dangerous than we thought," he said grimly. "But it could also be the key to understanding everything."

Evelyn nodded, feeling a renewed sense of purpose. The thought that they might uncover the truth about the Bermuda Triangle, about all the lives that had been lost here, gave her the strength to push forward. She had always been driven by the pursuit of knowledge, but now, it was more than that. It was about justice, about giving a voice to those who had vanished without a trace.

As they continued along the path, the environment around them began to change. The floating islands became more densely packed, forming a labyrinth of rock and crystal that twisted and turned in seemingly impossible ways. The air grew colder, and the light from the spire dimmed slightly, casting long, ominous shadows that seemed to move of their own accord.

The path led them into a narrow canyon, the walls towering high above them, covered in strange, luminescent plants that glowed with an otherworldly light. The air was thick with moisture, and the ground beneath their feet was slick and treacherous. The sense of being watched grew stronger, and Evelyn couldn't shake the feeling that they were walking into a trap.

"Stay alert," Captain Harris warned, his voice tense. "This place is too quiet. Something's not right."

Evelyn's heart raced as she scanned the canyon walls, looking for any sign of danger. The silence was oppressive, broken only by the soft rustle of the glowing plants as they swayed in an unseen breeze. The air was thick with tension, and every nerve in her body was on edge.

Suddenly, a low, rumbling sound echoed through the canyon, growing louder with each passing second. The ground beneath them began to tremble, and the walls of the canyon seemed to close in, the plants shivering and flickering with a sickly green light.

"What's happening?" Sarah cried; her voice high with panic.

Evelyn's mind raced as she tried to make sense of the situation. The rumbling grew louder, the ground shaking so violently that they could barely keep their footing. She glanced back at the spire, hoping for some kind of guidance, but the symbols on its surface were shifting too quickly to be read.

"Run!" Captain Harris shouted, his voice cutting through the chaos. "We need to get out of here, now!"

The team sprinted down the path, their breaths coming in ragged gasps as the canyon walls seemed to close in around them. The rumbling reached a deafening crescendo, and with a sickening crack, the ground split open behind them, revealing a yawning chasm that swallowed the path they had just crossed.

Evelyn's heart pounded in her chest as they ran, the chasm widening with each passing second. The plants along the canyon walls seemed to reach out towards them, their glowing tendrils pulsing with a malevolent light. The air was filled with a cacophony of sounds cracks, roars, and the eerie wail of the wind as it rushed through the narrow passage.

They were almost at the end of the canyon when the ground beneath Evelyn's feet gave way. She stumbled, her arms flailing as she tried to regain her balance, but the slick surface offered no grip. She felt herself falling, the chasm rushing up to meet her, when suddenly, a strong hand grabbed her arm, pulling her back to solid ground.

Collins yanked her to safety, his face pale and streaked with dirt. "I've got you!" he shouted over the noise, his grip tight as he helped her regain her footing.

Evelyn's heart raced as she stumbled forward, the chasm behind her widening with terrifying speed. The team burst out of the canyon just as the ground gave way entirely, the rumbling finally subsiding as the chasm sealed itself shut, leaving only a narrow ledge of safety behind them.

They collapsed onto the ground, gasping for breath, their hearts pounding in their chests. The danger had passed, but the terror of what they had just experienced lingered in the air, a tangible presence that weighed heavily on them.

"That was too close," Sarah whispered, her voice trembling as she hugged herself tightly. "I thought we were done for."

Evelyn nodded, her mind still reeling from the near-death experience. "Whatever this place is, it's fighting us," she said, her voice hoarse. "It doesn't want us to reach our destination."

Captain Harris pushed himself to his feet, his expression grim. "Then we're on the right track," he said, determination lacing his voice. "If this place is trying to stop us, it means we're getting closer to the truth. And that's exactly where we need to go."

Evelyn felt a surge of resolve at his words. He was right they had come too far to turn back now. The realm had thrown everything it had at them, but they had survived. And they would continue to survive, no matter what lay ahead.

As they stood up and prepared to continue, Evelyn cast one last glance back at the canyon, now silent and still.
The glowing plants had gone dark, their tendrils limp and lifeless. The danger had passed, but she knew it was only temporary. Whatever was waiting for them at the end of the path would be even more challenging, even more dangerous.

But they would face it together, as they always had. And no matter what happened, they would uncover the truth about this place and the Bermuda Triangle. The lives that had been lost here demanded nothing less.

With a deep breath, Evelyn turned towards the path ahead, the spire's light guiding them forward. The journey was far from over, but she was ready to face whatever lay ahead.

As they moved forward, the faint glow of the spire continued to pulse, a beacon of hope in the darkness. They were stepping into the unknown, but they were not afraid. They had each other, and they had a mission.

The Bermuda Triangle's mysteries would be unraveled, no matter the cost.

Chapter 20

The path ahead was narrower than before, winding through a landscape that grew increasingly alien with every step. The air was thick and heavy, as though it carried the weight of countless secrets and untold stories. The spire's light, once warm and reassuring, now flickered like a candle in a draft, casting eerie shadows that danced and shifted across the jagged terrain.

Evelyn led the way, her senses heightened, her mind racing with questions that refused to settle. The events of the canyon had shaken her deeply, the close brush with death leaving a lingering unease that gnawed at the edges of her thoughts. She could feel the realm's hostility more acutely now, a palpable force that seemed to press in from all sides, as though the very air was trying to smother them.

But there was something else, too an undercurrent of familiarity that she couldn't quite place. It was as if the realm was whispering to her, tugging at the corners of her memory, urging her to remember something just beyond her grasp. The sensation was disorienting, like trying to recall a dream that had already begun to fade upon waking.

"Do you feel that?" Sarah asked quietly, her voice breaking the heavy silence. She was walking close to Evelyn, her eyes wide and darting nervously at every shadow. "It's like… I don't know how to describe it. Like we're walking through someone's memories, or maybe our own."

Evelyn nodded, though she didn't fully understand it herself. "I feel it too. It's almost like déjà vu, but stronger. Like we've been here before, even though I know we haven't."

Collins, who had been following closely behind, frowned in thought. "I've read about places where time and space overlap, where different moments in history bleed into each other. Maybe that's what's happening here. We're experiencing echoes of the past, or maybe even the future."

Harris, ever the pragmatist, remained silent, but his grip on his weapon tightened. His eyes scanned the landscape with a sharp, analytical gaze, searching for any sign of danger. He was a man used to dealing with the tangible, the here and now, but even he couldn't ignore the strangeness that seemed to seep from every rock and shadow in this place.

As they continued, the path began to descend into a valley, the walls of which were lined with towering structures that resembled ancient ruins. The architecture was unlike anything they had ever seen an amalgamation of styles that seemed to span across different cultures and time periods. Some of the structures were crumbling and overgrown with strange, glowing vegetation, while others appeared eerily well-preserved, as if they had been frozen in time.

"This place is… it's impossible," Sarah whispered, her voice filled with awe and trepidation. "How can something like this exist? It's like a graveyard of forgotten civilizations."

Evelyn couldn't help but agree. The ruins were both haunting and mesmerizing, a testament to the countless lives that had been touched by this place, and perhaps lost to it. She felt a deep, almost overwhelming sadness as she looked at the structures, as though the weight of all those lost souls was pressing down on her, urging her to remember them, to understand their stories.

"This isn't just a realm," she said softly, more to herself than to the others. "It's a crossroads a place where time and space, life and death, all intersect. These ruins… they're pieces of different worlds, different times, all converging here."

Collins was silent for a moment, absorbing her words. "If that's true, then it means this place isn't just dangerous it's alive. It's feeding off these moments, these lives, and we're just the latest ones to get caught in its web."

Harris, who had been examining one of the more intact structures, turned back to the group, his expression grim. "Whatever this place is, it's not natural. We need to stay focused.

If it's trying to confuse us, it's doing a damn good job. But we can't afford to lose sight of our goal."

Evelyn nodded, though the disquiet in her heart only grew stronger. The path they were on felt less like a journey forward and more like a descent into a labyrinth of forgotten memories, each turn revealing another layer of the mystery that surrounded them.

As they walked, she noticed subtle changes in the environment. The air grew colder, the light dimmer. The ruins became more elaborate, more ornate, as though they were moving closer to the heart of the realm. The whispers that had once been at the edge of her consciousness grew louder, more insistent, and she found herself straining to understand them, even though she knew they weren't meant for her.

Suddenly, Evelyn stopped in her tracks, her breath catching in her throat. Ahead of them, at the center of the valley, stood a massive structure, far larger and more imposing than any they had seen so far. It was a pyramid, its surface covered in strange symbols that glowed with an eerie, pulsating light.

The symbols were like those on the spire, but more complex, more intricate, as though they held some deeper meaning that eluded her understanding.

"This must be it," Evelyn said, her voice barely above a whisper. "This is what the map was leading us to."

Sarah shivered beside her. "It feels… wrong. Like it's watching us, waiting for us to make a move."

Collins moved closer to Evelyn; his eyes locked on the pyramid. "If this is the heart of the realm, then whatever answers we're looking for are in there. But we need to be careful. We have no idea what we're walking into."

Evelyn nodded, her heart pounding in her chest. Every instinct screamed at her to turn back, to run as far and as fast as she could, but she knew that wasn't an option. They had come too far, and the answers they sought were too important.

Taking a deep breath, she took the first step towards the pyramid, her legs trembling with a mix of fear and determination. The others followed, their expressions tense, their movements cautious. The air around them seemed to hum with energy, the symbols on the pyramid growing brighter as they approached.

As they reached the base of the structure, the ground beneath their feet began to tremble, the vibrations growing stronger with each passing second. The symbols on the pyramid pulsed in time with the tremors, and Evelyn felt a strange sensation in her chest, as though her heart was being pulled in rhythm with the light.

"What's happening?" Sarah asked, her voice rising in panic as she stumbled back, clutching her chest.

Evelyn couldn't answer. The sensation was overwhelming, a force that seemed to draw her towards the pyramid with an almost magnetic pull. She reached out, her hand trembling as it brushed against the glowing surface.

The moment her fingers made contact, the world around her exploded in light.

She was no longer standing in the valley. Instead, she found herself in a vast, endless void, the only sound the pounding of her heart in her ears. The light from the pyramid surrounded her, wrapping around her like a cocoon, and she felt herself being pulled deeper into the void, further and further from her companions, from the realm, from everything.

She tried to scream, to call out for help, but no sound came from her throat. Panic surged through her, but it was quickly drowned out by a wave of memories that weren't her own, memories that flooded her mind with images and sensations she couldn't begin to comprehend.

She saw flashes of people, men, women, children walking through the valley, just as she and her team had done. Some were dressed in ancient robes, others in modern clothing, but all of them shared the same look of fear and confusion that she had seen in her own team's eyes. She saw them approach the pyramid, just as she had, and she watched as each of them reached out to touch it, just as she had done.

And then she saw what happened next.

Each person was consumed by the light, their forms dissolving into nothingness as they were pulled into the void. Their screams echoed in her mind, their terror and pain searing into her consciousness. She felt their fear, their desperation, as they were stripped of their identities, their memories, their very essence.

But it didn't stop there. The memories continued to flood her mind, each one more horrific than the last. She saw battles fought on distant worlds, civilizations rising and falling, all of them connected to this place, all of them drawn into the same endless cycle of destruction and rebirth.

And at the center of it all was the pyramid, the heart of the realm, the source of its power. It was ancient, far older than anything she could comprehend, and it was alive. It fed on the lives it claimed, absorbing their memories, their experiences, their very souls, and using them to fuel its own existence.

Evelyn's mind reeled as she struggled to make sense of what she was seeing. The pyramid wasn't just a structure, it was a being, a consciousness that had existed for eons, feeding off the lives of those who entered its domain. And it was hungry, always hungry for more.

She felt it reaching out to her, its tendrils of light wrapping around her mind, probing, searching for a way in. It wanted her memories, her experiences, her soul, and it wouldn't stop until it had consumed her completely.

"No!" Evelyn screamed, the word tearing from her throat with a force that shocked her. She wasn't going to let it take her, she wasn't going to become another victim of this place.

Summoning every ounce of strength she had left, she fought back against the pull of the pyramid, pushing it out of her mind with a force of will she didn't know she possessed. The light around her flickered, dimmed, and then shattered like glass, the void collapsing in on itself as she was thrown back into the realm.

She landed hard on the ground, gasping for breath as the world around her came back into focus. The pyramid loomed above her, its light now dims and flickering, as though it had been weakened by her resistance.

"Evelyn!" Collins was at her side in an instant, his hands on her shoulders, his face pale with fear. "What happened? Are you okay?"

She nodded, though she wasn't sure she was. Her mind was a whirlwind of emotions and images, the memories she had witnessed still fresh in her mind. But she was alive, and that was all that mattered.

"We have to destroy it," she said, her voice hoarse but filled with determination. "That pyramid... it's the source of all of this.

It's feeding on the lives it takes, and it won't stop until it's destroyed."

Harris, who had been watching the pyramid warily, nodded in agreement. "Then that's what we'll do. We'll find a way to bring it down."

Sarah, still shaken but resolute, stepped forward. "How? It's not like we can just blow it up. There must be something else, something that can weaken it."

Evelyn thought back to the memories she had seen, the endless cycle of destruction and rebirth. "It's connected to the lives it's taken. If we can find a way to release those souls, to break its connection to them, we might be able to weaken it enough to destroy it."

Collins frowned. "But how do we do that? We don't even know where to start."

Evelyn looked up at the pyramid, its light now barely more than a faint glow. "We start by going inside. Whatever power it has, it's coming from within. If we can find the source, we can stop it."

Harris nodded, his expression grim. "Then let's do it. But we move carefully. We don't know what we're walking into."

Evelyn stood; her legs still shaky but her resolve stronger than ever. They had come to this place seeking answers, but now they were fighting for something far greater. The pyramid had taken too many lives, and it was time to put an end to its reign of terror.

With one last glance at her team, Evelyn led the way towards the entrance of the pyramid, her heart pounding in her chest. The path ahead was dark and uncertain, but she knew one thing for sure: they would not be the next victims of this place. They would survive, and they would destroy the pyramid, no matter the cost.

As they stepped into the darkness of the pyramid, the light of the spire fading behind them, Evelyn couldn't shake the feeling that they were walking into a trap. But it didn't matter. They had a mission, and they would see it through to the end. The Bermuda Triangle's secrets would be unravelled, and the lives lost to its power would finally find peace.

Chapter 21

The entrance of the pyramid was a yawning black maw, its darkness impenetrable even by the faint light that flickered weakly from the symbols etched into its surface. As Evelyn stepped forward, her pulse quickened, every nerve in her body screaming a warning. The air inside the pyramid was thick and suffocating, a far cry from the humid, salty air outside. It was as if the structure itself exhaled an oppressive force, a presence that sought to crush them under its immense weight.

"Stay close," Captain Harris commanded, his voice taut with tension. His usual stoic demeanor was strained, as if even he couldn't entirely dismiss the foreboding that clung to the very walls of the pyramid.

The team followed Evelyn, their footsteps echoing ominously in the cavernous space. The interior of the pyramid was a labyrinth of stone corridors and narrow passages, each one seeming to twist and spiral in ways that defied logic. The walls were covered in the same glowing symbols, but here they pulsated with a sickly, greenish light that cast eerie, shifting patterns on their faces.

Every step felt like a descent deeper into the heart of something malevolent. Evelyn's mind was a storm of thoughts, the memories from the void still fresh, their images seared into her consciousness. She could feel the souls of those lost to the pyramid thousands, perhaps millions pressing against the thin veil of reality, desperate to be freed, to be remembered.

But there was something else gnawing at her, something darker. She couldn't shake the sensation that the pyramid was aware of them, that it was watching them, waiting for them to make a mistake. Each twist in the path felt like a deliberate misdirection, a trap set by an unseen hand.

"What do you think we'll find?" Sarah's voice broke through Evelyn's reverie, trembling with barely restrained fear. "What if there's nothing? What if we can't stop it?"

Evelyn hesitated, glancing back at Sarah. She could see the fear etched on her friend's face, a reflection of her own anxieties. But she couldn't afford to let doubt creep in, not now, when they were so close.

"We'll find something," Evelyn said, forcing a note of certainty into her voice. "The pyramid has a source of power, and if we can reach it, we can destroy it. We must believe that."

But even as she spoke, the words felt hollow. How could they, a small team of humans, hope to defeat something so ancient, so incomprehensibly powerful? The very thought felt absurd, but she knew there was no turning back.

As they ventured deeper, the corridors began to narrow, the walls pressing in on them. The light from the symbols grew brighter, almost blinding, and the air became thick with a cloying, metallic scent that turned Evelyn's stomach. She could feel a low hum vibrating through the stone beneath her feet, like the pulse of a living creature.

"Do you hear that?" Collins whispered, his voice barely audible over the hum. His eyes were wide, his normally calm demeanor cracked by the growing tension.

Evelyn nodded, the sound reverberating through her bones. It was a low, constant thrumming, a vibration that seemed to originate from deep within the pyramid, resonating through the stone and into their very bodies. It wasn't just a sound—it was a sensation, a physical manifestation of the pyramid's power.

"It's like it's alive," Sarah murmured, her voice trembling. "This place... it's more than just a structure. It's... it's a being."

Evelyn didn't respond. She didn't have to. They all felt it the presence that seemed to grow stronger with every step they took. The pyramid wasn't just a building; it was a living, breathing entity, feeding off the fear and desperation of those who entered it.

As they reached a wide, circular chamber at the center of the pyramid, the source of the hum became apparent. In the center of the room stood a massive, obsidian monolith, its surface etched with the same glowing symbols that covered the walls. The monolith pulsed with a deep, crimson light, the intensity of which seemed to match the pounding of Evelyn's heart.

"This is it," Evelyn said, her voice barely above a whisper. "This is the source."

The room felt like it was vibrating, the walls pulsing in rhythm with the monolith's light. The air was so thick with tension that it was almost tangible, a heavy, oppressive force that pressed down on them, making it difficult to breathe.

Captain Harris approached the monolith cautiously, his eyes narrowed as he examined the symbols. "These markings... they're like the ones we saw on the spire, but they're more complex. It's like they're a language, a code, maybe."

Evelyn moved closer, her eyes scanning the symbols. As she stared at them, they seemed to shift and change, the lines and curves rearranging themselves into patterns that were both familiar and alien. She could almost understand them, as if they were speaking directly to her, bypassing the need for translation.

"It's like they're alive," she said, her voice tinged with awe and fear. "They're trying to communicate with us."

"Or control us," Collins added grimly. "This thing has been feeding off the lives of everyone who's ever come here. It's not just a power source.... it's a predator."

The realization hit Evelyn like a cold wave. The monolith wasn't just a machine; it was a living entity, an ancient, malevolent force that had consumed countless souls over the eons. And now, it was trying to consume them.

"We need to destroy it," Evelyn said, her voice firm. "Before it can do the same to us."

But how? The question hung in the air, unspoken but undeniable. How could they hope to destroy something so powerful, so ancient?

Suddenly, the ground beneath their feet began to tremble, the vibrations growing stronger with each passing second. The walls of the chamber pulsed with a brilliant light, the symbols glowing brighter and brighter until they were nearly blinding.

The monolith's hum grew louder, a deep, resonant sound that shook the very air. The symbols on its surface began to move, shifting and rearranging themselves in a pattern that made Evelyn's head spin.

"It's reacting to us," Sarah cried out, panic rising in her voice. "We have to do something, now!"

Evelyn's mind raced as she tried to think of a solution. They needed to stop the monolith, but how? It was too powerful, too deeply entrenched in the fabric of the realm.

Unless...

An idea began to form in her mind, a wild, desperate idea that might just be their only chance. She remembered the memories she had seen in the void, the countless lives that had been consumed by the pyramid, their souls trapped within its walls. If the monolith was feeding off those souls, then perhaps they could use that connection against it.

"What if we could sever the connection?" Evelyn said, turning to the others. "What if we could free the souls that it's trapped, weaken it from the inside?"

Collins frowned. "How do we do that? We don't have the tools, the technology."

"We have our minds," Evelyn interrupted, her voice filled with conviction. "We've seen what this place can do. It can reach into our thoughts, our memories. Maybe we can do the same reach out to the souls that are trapped here, help them break free."

The others stared at her; uncertainty etched on their faces. It was a long shot, a wild gamble, but it was the only option they had left.

"We don't have time to debate this," Captain Harris said, his voice steady. "If we're going to do this, we need to do it now."

Evelyn nodded, her heart pounding in her chest. "Everyone, focus. Think about the souls that are trapped here, the lives that have been lost. Reach out to them, call to them. We need to show them the way out."

The team closed their eyes, their faces tense with concentration. Evelyn could feel the energy in the room shifting, the vibrations of the monolith growing more erratic as they focused their minds.

She reached out with her thoughts, imagining a door, a gateway through which the trapped souls could escape. She could feel them now, the countless lives that had been consumed by the pyramid, their fear and pain echoing through her mind.

"We're here to help you," she whispered, her voice trembling with emotion. "We're going to set you free."

The light from the monolith flared, a blinding flash that seared through the chamber. Evelyn gasped as she felt the souls reaching out to her, their desperation and hope mingling with her own.

And then, something incredible happened. The symbols on the monolith began to fade, their light dimming as the connection between the pyramid and the trapped souls began to break. The air in the chamber grew lighter, the oppressive weightlifting as the souls began to slip free, their energy flooding the room with a warmth that chased away the cold, metallic chill.

The monolith shuddered, its surface cracking as the energy that had sustained it for eons began to drain away. The hum that had filled the chamber faded into silence, replaced by a soft, gentle breeze that whispered through the room.

Evelyn opened her eyes, tears streaming down her face as she felt the souls departing, their presence a gentle caress that filled her with a sense of peace and relief. The monolith, once a towering, malevolent presence, was now nothing more than a cracked, lifeless husk.

"It's over," Sarah whispered, her voice filled with awe. "We did it."

But Evelyn knew better. This was only the beginning. The pyramid's power had been weakened, but it wasn't destroyed. Not yet. They had won a battle, but the war was far from over. As they stood in the chamber, the remnants of the monolith crumbling to dust around them, Evelyn knew that their fight was not just against the pyramid, but against the very force that had created it. A force that was ancient, powerful, and far from defeated.

But for the first time since they had entered the Bermuda Triangle, she felt a spark of hope. They had weakened the pyramid, and in doing so, they had given themselves a chance. A chance to destroy the pyramid once and for all, to free the Bermuda Triangle from its grip and to save countless lives from its wrath.

As they prepared to leave the chamber, Evelyn glanced back at the remnants of the monolith. The souls were free, their voices now silent, but their presence lingered, a comforting reminder that they were not alone in this fight.

"We're going to finish this," she whispered to herself, her resolve stronger than ever. "No matter what it takes."

With that, she turned and led the team out of the chamber, their steps lighter, their hearts filled with determination. The Bermuda Triangle had taken so much from them, but they were not defeated. Not yet. And as long as they had breath in their bodies, they would fight.

Chapter 22

The sun began its slow ascent, casting long shadows across the remnants of the Bermuda Triangle's dreaded pyramid. Evelyn's body ached with exhaustion, but a profound sense of relief surged through her as she watched the once-menacing structure crumble into a pile of rubble. The island seemed to breathe a collective sigh of relief, as if it, too, had been waiting for this moment.

As the helicopter approached the shore, the world below appeared eerily calm, a stark contrast to the chaos they had just escaped. Evelyn's mind was a maelstrom of thoughts and emotions. The pyramid's destruction had been a victory, but the cost weighed heavily on her. The memories of the battles fought, the souls freed, and the near-death experiences played like a relentless reel in her mind. Each moment was etched into her consciousness, a reminder of their journey through the abyss.

Inside the helicopter, the team sat in silence, each lost in their private contemplation. Collins, his face smeared with dirt and blood, looked out the window, his expression a mixture of disbelief and satisfaction. "I never thought I'd see the end of this," he said quietly, almost to himself. His voice was raspy, a reflection of the strain they had endured. "I thought we were done for more than once."

Evelyn met his gaze, offering a weary smile. "We made it. We're here." Her own voice was strained, betraying the emotional and physical toll the ordeal had taken. She knew the journey had left its mark on all of them, and the emotional weight was almost as heavy as the physical exhaustion.

Sarah, seated across from Evelyn, clutched her arms around herself as if trying to hold onto some semblance of normalcy. Her eyes, red and puffy, reflected the turmoil she had experienced. She glanced at Evelyn, her voice trembling. "What if it wasn't enough? What if there's something we missed?"

Evelyn reached out and placed a reassuring hand on Sarah's arm. "We did everything we could. We faced the heart of the pyramid; we fought the darkness. We've weakened its grip on this place. The fact that we're here, alive, means we did something right."

Sarah nodded, though doubt lingered in her eyes. Evelyn understood the sentiment. It was hard to shake off the fear that their victory might be temporary, that the darkness they had faced might find a way to return. But Evelyn tried to push those thoughts aside, focusing instead on the tangible evidence of their success the crumbling ruins below, the absence of the pyramid's oppressive energy.

Harris, his face set in a grim expression of determination, turned his gaze towards the horizon. The sun's light was slowly warming the ocean, the surface glittering like a sea of diamonds. "It's hard to believe it's finally over," he said. "The pyramid is destroyed, but there's still so much to process."

Evelyn could feel the weight of his words. The destruction of the pyramid was a monumental achievement, but it came with its own set of challenges. They had faced something ancient and powerful, something that had shaped the world's myths and fears. Now, they had to reconcile their experiences with the reality of returning to their lives.

The helicopter touched down on the deck of the ship, the familiar surroundings a stark contrast to the chaos they had left behind. As they disembarked, the ship's crew gathered around them, their faces reflecting a mixture of awe and relief. The sight of the team, battered and bruised but alive, stirred a sense of disbelief and admiration among the onlookers.

Captain Reynolds, his face a mask of concern, approached them.

"What happened down there?" he asked, his voice carrying a note of disbelief. "Is it really over?"

Evelyn looked at the captain, her emotions a complex blend of relief and exhaustion. "Yes," she replied. "The pyramid is destroyed. The Bermuda Triangle's threat is gone."

The captain's eyes widened in astonishment. "I can hardly believe it. You've done something incredible."

Evelyn nodded, though she felt far from incredible. She felt tired, overwhelmed by the gravity of their journey and the emotional toll it had taken. "We've done what we set out to do," she said softly. "But there's still much work to be done. We need to ensure that the story of what happened here is told, that the world knows the truth."

As they made their way to the ship's quarters, Evelyn took a moment to herself, leaning against the railing and staring out at the sea. The ocean's vast expanse was a calming presence, a reminder of the world's endless possibilities and the freedom they had fought so hard to reclaim.

Her thoughts drifted back to the pyramid, to the souls they had freed, and to the harrowing battles they had faced. Each moment was a thread in the tapestry of their journey, woven together into a story of courage and perseverance. She thought of the people who had suffered because of the pyramid, their voices now silent but their presence felt in the echoes of their liberation.

A soft touch on her shoulder brought Evelyn back to the present. She turned to find Sarah standing beside her, her eyes filled with gratitude. "Thank you," Sarah said softly. "For everything. I don't know if we would have made it without you."

Evelyn managed a tired smile. "We made it together. That's what matters."

As they settled into their quarters, the ship began its journey back to the nearest port. The crew worked diligently, their movements a testament to their relief and their respect for the team's achievement. The sun was setting, casting a warm, golden light across the water, and Evelyn felt a sense of peace settling over her.

The days at sea were a time of reflection and healing. The team slowly began to recover, their bodies and minds gradually returning to normal. They shared stories of their experiences, talked through their fears, and began to rebuild the connections that had been strained by their ordeal.

Evelyn found solace in these conversations, in the shared moments of vulnerability and triumph. She realized that their journey had not only changed the world but had also changed them. They were no longer just survivors; they were a team bound by a profound experience, their bonds strengthened by their shared struggles and victories.

As the ship neared the port, Evelyn felt a surge of anticipation. They were returning to a world that had been untouched by the darkness they had faced, but they were not the same people who had left. They had seen the edge of something ancient and powerful, and they had emerged victorious.

When they finally docked and disembarked, they were greeted by a world that seemed both familiar and new. The bustling port was a stark contrast to the isolation of the Bermuda Triangle, a reminder of the life they were returning to. The sun shone brightly, and the air was filled with the sounds of life, a reminder that they were once again part of a world that was moving forward.

Evelyn took a deep breath, her heart filled with a mixture of relief and hope. The Bermuda Triangle was no longer a place of fear and darkness. It was a place of memories, of battles fought and won, and of a journey that had changed their lives forever.

As the team prepared to go their separate ways, Evelyn knew that they would carry the experiences of their journey with them. They had faced the darkness and had emerged into the light, and that light would guide them in the days to come.

The journey had been long and arduous, but it had also been a testament to their courage and determination. They had faced the worst and had come out stronger, their spirits unbroken and their hearts full of hope.

Evelyn looked at her team, her friends, and felt a profound sense of gratitude. They had shared something extraordinary, and that shared experience had forged a bond that would last a lifetime.

The Bermuda Triangle was behind them, but the future was filled with possibilities. And as Evelyn stepped onto the shore, ready to face whatever lay ahead, she knew that they were ready to meet it with the same strength and courage that had seen them through the darkest days.

The world was different now, and so were they. The journey had changed them, but it had also given them a new purpose, a new understanding of themselves and their place in the world.

And as they walked away from the port, leaving the past behind, Evelyn felt a sense of peace and accomplishment. They had faced the darkness and had emerged victorious. They had done what few could even imagine, and they had done it together.

The Bermuda Triangle was no longer a place of fear. It was a place of lessons learned and triumphs celebrated. And as Evelyn looked towards the horizon, she knew that the future held both challenges and opportunities.

But no matter what lay ahead, they would face it together, with the same courage and determination that had seen them through their darkest hour. They were ready for whatever came next, and they were ready to embrace the future with open hearts and unbreakable spirits.

The journey had ended, but the adventure was just beginning.